Challenger

Other Books by Patsey Gray:

Heads Up
Doggone Roan
4-H Filly
Galloping Gold

Challenger

BY PATSEY GRAY

ILLUSTRATED BY SAM SAVITT

COWARD-MCCANN, INC.

NEW YORK

© 1959 by Coward-McCann, Inc.

Library of Congress
Catalog Card Number: 59–11435

MANUFACTURED IN THE UNITED STATES OF AMERICA

Contents

Challenger

1. Address: Fairgrounds

---

*S*HE was a lucky girl, Ellie realized, to be leading almost exactly the life she wanted. This minute, for instance, here she was riding into the ring on Challenger. Hardly any hour of the twenty-four was as nice as now, seven o'clock on a June morning. No place surely was as exciting as a show ring, especially when you were schooling for a Hunt Seat Medal. And no hunter in the whole world equaled her own Challenger, as far as Ellie Sayre was concerned.

"Wait," she said to him, pausing at the ring's entrance. "Let's see who's schooling this morning." There weren't many, for not many exhibitors arrived a whole week before the show. Only the professionals like herself and her grandfather, whose business brought them here; and people who could afford to stay at the swank motels near Palm Springs to enjoy the California sunshine. Among the last group were the Mortons, who would arrive today. Ellie had a hunch that Pamela Morton was going to be Grandpa's most troublesome pupil.

Compared to the motels Grandpa's house trailer was pretty cramped. Still, it was cosy, with the bunk beds in Ellie's end, a tiny shower in the middle opposite the closet, and the kitchen-dinette in Grandpa's end, where you entered. There the couch served at night as his bed. The folding table was used for meals, and the ice box and butane stove were used to prepare them. At least the small size of their home on wheels meant less house-keeping. Ellie had enough of that anyway, because Grandpa always wanted the place kept neat.

Actually her chores were easy, but less fun than out-door work. Any girl in seventh grade should be able to sweep, dust, mend and iron. Ellie didn't have to wash, thanks to the launderettes in every town. It was Grandpa who had the really big task, cooking. The one fault she found with the trailer was that it was her home only in summer. Because of school, she had to spend the rest of the year in town, with her parents and sisters. She loved them of course, and luckily they lived near Grandpa's training stables in South San Francisco, his winter quarters. But those months at home were dull compared to the summer ones. Almost desperately she looked forward all year to summer vacation and her job on the show circuit.

"Hi, El, c'mon in!" It was one of her rivals, hailing her from inside the ring as she sat her big horse by the gate.

Urging Challenger forward, Ellie began circling at a walk after answering hello to the Rawlings boy. She couldn't help liking him, as everyone did. He was so good natured that he didn't mind being called "Rolly," a name due partly to his shape and partly to how often he rolled off his mounts. But she didn't chat now with Rolly or anyone else. Her grandfather didn't allow "visiting" during work.

"If you want to play, play somewhere else," he would say. "If you want to work, that's different. I'll help you all I can. I believe you have the makings of a rider, maybe of a future trainer." Here he would smile a little sadly. "But I haven't as much future left as you, so don't waste my time. Also don't spoil my reputation as a teacher, or we may go hungry. For both our sakes, I'm hoping you'll be my best advertisement."

Ellie decided that according to schedule she had walked Challenger long enough. She shortened the reins, shoved down her heels and tightened her long blue-jeaned legs. Knowing her so well, Challenger took up the trot before she asked him to. That would mean a black mark for her from Grandpa! He wanted to see her being boss, not Challenger. She hoped, but doubted, that he had taken his sharp blue eyes off her for a moment, wherever he sat in the grandstand. He would be alone by choice, in order to concentrate. He never schooled her from the ringside, shouting orders like some trainers. He gave orders ahead of time, then quietly watched her perform. Later he praised or criticized her in private.

Now she held her chin up, as he had taught her, and remembered about her back, hands, elbows, shoulders, legs and feet. There were so many things to think of all at once! She glanced down and saw that her hold on the reins was just right, her wrists supple.

Under her, Challenger was swinging along at a steady trot, his stride rhythmic, muscles pumping beneath the shining chestnut coat. That coat should shine all right, Ellie thought, after all the brushing and rubbing she had given it. His ears were pricked, one then the other flicking back for her voice. He knew what to expect, because he was almost as familiar with the routine as she was. And then he was smarter than most horses. He really *thought*.

"Time to canter," she told him after four laps of the ring. There were few riders today, which meant he would be able to stay on the rail. Only a couple of

fellows were jumping, so there was no danger of colli-
sions.

Ellie pulled down to a walk, collected her horse and
rocked off into a canter. She was pretty sure she hadn't
given any visible aids, which should please Grandpa.
He maintained that one way to spot a beginner was his
exaggerated signals. Also by the overuse of whip and
spurs. It was better not to use these at all unless a rider
was expert. If he was, then he should know how to
apply them when discipline was necessary. After all,
said Grandpa, you shouldn't spoil a horse, any more
than you would a child.

As usual, at the canter Challenger was taking a good
hold. Ellie hoped this wasn't one of the days he felt too
terribly strong. "Oh come on now," she coaxed. "Be
nice, will you? Please, honey." He settled into a more
controlled pace. She was able to enjoy the wind of
motion against her face, lifting her bangs. She smelled
the lovely bitter odor of tanbark and tasted it in the dry
air. She forgot the other horsemen and heard only the
muffled hoofbeats of Challenger, his snorty blowing,
which he did when he felt good. He felt good the same
way she did—strong and successful, happy because they
were together. She knew exactly all the time how he
felt and what he was thinking. Nobody could persuade
her she didn't, though people teased her about her claim

that she and Challenger understood each other perfectly. Now out of pure pleasure she smiled to herself and met the rush of air cold against the metal retainer on her teeth.

It was time to pull up and reverse. She didn't have to look down to make sure of being on the correct lead. She had long ago learned to tell by feel, as she could also tell if his lead was right behind or if he was cross cantering. But she couldn't resist one more satisfied glance at her hands on the reins.

Four laps this way and she pulled in, looking for her grandfather. He would come in now to set up the jumps, maybe raising or lowering them. Only two today, he'd said. "Two, with no mistakes." She watched him walk in, a tall thin man in worn but neat britches and boots, with a cap over his gray hair. Bowlegged he might be, but his body was straight and his mind as sharp as if he were still a cavalry sergeant. Her parents said that his army training explained his precise ways, his belief in discipline.

Using the white poles and standards, he fixed a post-and-rails at one side of the ring. At the other he indicated the brush jump. Both were about three foot six. Ellie suspected that in placing these two fences so simply he was purposely giving Challenger a change of course to keep him on his toes. In the medal class the jumps would be arranged in a figure eight, and that was the way he had been setting them lately—much trickier than today. He watched her check her girth, then nodded "Go ahead." He wasn't going to repeat directions already given. It was up to her to carry them out.

Deliberately she had Challenger break off into a canter, heading for the brush, since that was normally the first fence on any course. He wasn't rushing, but wasn't hanging back either. From way off he was watching his fence, suiting his stride to the distance, then measuring his take off, gathering himself, and— now! He was up and over and on, all in one flowing motion, while she leaned forward, giving him rein, then righted herself to take back around the corner. But darn it, he was taking back himself. "You might as well have no rider!" she exclaimed in annoyance. "It's easy for Grandpa to say I must boss you, but how can I when you do everything right, and know more than I do?" It was the same over the post and rails. No mistakes, as far as she could see. The simple course hadn't fooled Challenger into forgetting what he knew.

Back in the center, Grandpa's "That'll do" told her he was satisfied. He might have said something nice, only he never did believe in useless compliments. It was Rolly Rawlings, sitting his horse to watch, who called, "Good goin', El." He added, "The girl with the shining smile!" He was teasing her about her retainer. That reminded her it was making her teeth ache, so she took it off and pocketed it.

A few minutes later at Barn B she dismounted and unsaddled. Now she must cool Challenger, pick out his feet, rub him down and feed him breakfast. And she would talk with him a few minutes to keep him encouraged, for he needed lots of confidence. Then she would have her own breakfast with Grandpa while he commented on her performance and gave her the day's instructions. This was always one of the best hours, and about the only one they could enjoy uninterrupted, for a professional trainer couldn't avoid his customers. Luckily, most of them didn't appear till later in the day.

She stepped into the trailer through Grandpa's end, where he had unfolded the table and was dishing up eggs and bacon and fruit. Washing in the miniature bathroom, Ellie could smell coffee mingled with outdoor smells, almost like camping. What finer spot to camp could there be than here at the end of Barn B farthest from the ring, right at the edge of a palm grove? Facing this barn across a dirt aisle was Barn C, and behind that were other barns. They were long sheds of connecting stalls, really not barn-shaped at all, running from the ring area to the palm grove. At this end of the shed row, Grandpa used the last electric outlet to plug in his extension cord. This gave the trailer light and power for appliances such as the iron, toaster, percolator and so on. Days were cool here, dimmed by the trees. At night Ellie could hear their fronds rustling, and horses shifting or munching, and distant sounds from the carnival that was part of this county fair. Best of all, it was easy to talk back and forth with Challenger, who had the very end stall nearest the trailer. Summer was a heavenly time, thought Ellie, when they moved from show to show, their address always: Fairgrounds, such and such a county.

Ellie sat down opposite Grandpa, eager to hear what he would say about her schooling.

But his first words were, "Your retainer, Ellen."

She fished it out and slipped it on. "How did you like our performance?" she asked.

"I had to score you two black marks," he replied.

"Two?" she protested. "I know I let Challenger decide when to trot, but what was the other for?"

"Twice I saw you admiring your hands."

He would see that! And after he had told her about a million times always to look ahead. She knew he didn't understand how anyone could forget as much as she did. His mind worked by law and order. Yet underneath, he was the kindest person. In his gay spells his Irish accent would come back and he would tell stories about when he was a lad, "with an eye for the girls and a way with a horse."

Drinking her milk, Ellie tried to explain the difficulty of bossing Challenger when he was already doing everything right.

Her grandfather listened thoughtfully while he ate. Then with one of his rare smiles he said, "Don't you realize that it's due to you that he does things right?" The smile crinkled his blue eyes, so like hers, and tightened the wrinkles in his tanned face. "In a way you've created the difficulty yourself, by working with him so patiently and restoring his confidence. Remember how frightened he was, so crazy that poor Mrs. Orville had to give him away?"

"Do I!" Ellie said. "Whoever she'd had taking care of him must have been mean as anything. Like Bull Johnson, always using his whip and swearing and hollering at his horses and jerking their mouths."

"Yes, you can't knock a thoroughbred around like that," Grandpa said soberly. "Especially not when you're handling him for a middle-aged amateur lady like Mrs. Orville."

Ellie remembered how she had been almost sick with happiness that she had been given the big handsome hunter with his four white stockings and the white diamond on his forehead. How marvelous that Mrs. Orville had seen enough of the Sayres to decide they were the ones most likely to be both kind and successful with Challenger. Successful, that is, if anyone could ever again get him calmed down. Grandpa hadn't been at all sure it would be possible. Ellie could try, he had said. If it didn't work . . . The question of what would happen to Challenger if it didn't work had never been settled. The main trouble was that he was so sensitive. Praise or blame made him either terribly happy or terribly unhappy.

For over a year Ellie had worked with Challenger, in summer on the circuit, in winter in town at Grandpa's stables. Even her parents hadn't guessed the hopes and despairs of such a project. Only she could know how hard she had struggled, and how slowly she had begun to succeed. Only Grandpa knew, or said, how both her horsemanship and character had improved in the effort. And only Challenger knew how a horse felt as he gradually—oh, so gradually—regained some confidence in people. Rather, in one person. He would still flinch and tremble at a shout or the crack of a whip, and he was wary of men, even of Grandpa. He accepted women less suspiciously, but it was Ellie alone whom he finally learned to trust.

Relaxing briefly after breakfast, Grandpa outlined the day's plans while Ellie cleared the table. Since the show wouldn't start for a week, she had no manes and tails to braid, therefore no earnings from her steadiest source. She would be mostly helping Grandpa, who expected two of his clients to arrive shortly with their horses. Then, there would be errands and odd jobs of exercising and cooling horses for the stables already here. With such a light schedule, Ellie could devote extra time to housecleaning, Grandpa suggested, and she groaned.

"These windows need washing," he pointed out. "The bathroom linoleum needs scrubbing, some of your clothes need repairs, and our silver needs polishing, if you're ambitious."

"I'm not that ambitious," she murmured, but he went right on.

"Chiefly I'll want your help this week with our new customers, the Mortons. They're due today, you know."

Of course, the Mortons. Ellie wondered how she could have forgotten them even temporarily. So many letters had passed between her grandfather and Pamela Morton's father that anyone would have thought the Queen of England was coming, at least! Ellie suspected Grandpa would have turned Pamela down as too much trouble, if it weren't for the pay.

While she washed the dishes, she tried again to picture Pamela. Pamela was rich, lived in Los Angeles, and wanted coaching for the medal classes. That much Ellie knew. She knew too that it was because of Grandpa's fine reputation that Pamela and her hunter were being entrusted to him. Once or twice at other horse shows Ellie had seen the girl on the flashy black mare, Night Flight. Not being concerned then, she had noticed only that Pamela was pretty and a good rider. Now it seemed that an interesting problem was being thrust on Grandpa. "Very, very interesting," Ellie told herself with a wicked grin. It appeared that Pamela was in a phase of mad passions for movie actors, and wanted to be an actress herself. This might be all right in the future, but hardly in seventh grade! In Mr. Morton's last letter, quoted by Grandpa, her father had sounded disgusted with what he called her airs and graces. Her parents were trying to shift her interests. Since she liked to jump they had persuaded her to compete for a medal. Her reward would be the trip to New York if she made the finals, for they were held each November in Madison Square Garden.

From all this and other things Ellie had heard, she was pretty sure Pamela was spoiled and headstrong— a real handful in fact. Now the interesting part was that so far Grandpa had been easily able to handle any handful. She thought of his eyes, which could chill like ice; of his tall figure, at times forbidding; of his voice, always controlled but frequently stern. Satisfied customers said it was partly his strictness which made him such a good teacher. But he had plenty of rivals too, other trainers who were just waiting to point out, "Patrick Sayre's getting too old for the job. He's slipping. He's finished."

Ellie didn't know about this Pamela, but no one

would say that because of *her*, she thought fiercely. She would do her absolute top best to win a medal, for Grandpa's sake as well as for Challenger's and her own. She knew it was likely that she would win. She couldn't help hearing flattering comments on her riding, and she knew Grandpa was being purposely restrained when he said only, "You have the makings of a rider." But if she did win, she would have to miss competing in the finals. Traveling to New York with a horse was an expense her family couldn't possibly afford. In a way it was easier to give up something completely out of reach than something for which there was hope. Of course, a person could dream . . .

In the bathroom again, cleaning her hateful retainer, she stared at her face in the small mirror. Blue eyes, snub nose, freckles, and boy-cut hair that insisted on sticking out in front like a thatched roof. How would Pamela like her? And how would she like Pamela?

She spoke to her reflection with mischief in her voice, "Something tells me it's not going to be at all dull around here. Not at all!"

2. The First Battle

By evening the day of Pamela's arrival, Ellie had about decided that her guess had been wrong. So far Pam had given no trouble. On the contrary, she was polite and attentive with Grandpa, who obviously was well impressed by her. Ellie chuckled to herself as she watched him falling for Pam, so to speak. He, who rarely complimented anyone, observed that Pam was a "charming girl, and mighty pretty." There was proof that his "eye for a girl" had not been dimmed by time! Yet, even while Ellie accused herself of being mean, she couldn't get rid of a lingering suspicion. Anyone who could turn on the charm as Pam did could probably turn it off too, and fast.

Now, while the summer dusk fell, the two girls were waiting for Pam's parents to fetch her. They had dropped her here after lunch, had chatted with

Grandpa, and left to check in at the motel. Their motel was "The Date Tree," an elegant place which Ellie had noticed, with a swimming pool, a lounging terrace and an open view over the desert.

Pam hadn't ridden this afternoon, although Ellie urged her to, wanting to study both Pam's horsemanship and her mare, Night Flight.

"Oh, I'll wait till morning," Pam said. "Let's let Flight relax and settle down." Grandpa agreed, for he saw that the young mare was a bit fussy in her new surroundings.

Ellie leaned on the half door of the box stall to inspect Flight. She certainly was a beauty. A little light-boned maybe, compared to Challenger, but with a classy head and a fine-haired glossy coat that showed breeding. Along with her had come a trunk full of expensive equipment. Ellie was thrilled just to examine the beautiful English double bridle, the polished curb and snaffle bits, fresh white folded rubrags, the brush, comb, foot hook, scraper and sponges. There was even a compartment in the trunk which held practically a drug store of salves and liniments, bandages, tape and cotton. From memory, she pictured Pam's show clothes: buff colored britches, gleaming black boots, well tailored coat, stock, gloves and black hunting cap. She wasn't especially envious. Those clothes would be nice to have, but no more serviceable than her own jodhpurs and jodhpur boots, her plain shirts and ties, an outfit like the one Pam wore now. In the ring Ellie wore a checked jacket, which this year was getting tight. She did have a hunting cap, kept in tissue paper, in a box under her bunk. What made it most valuable was that she had earned it, braiding manes and tails last summer till at times her fingers ached. She even braided in her dreams, or nightmares—horses twenty hands high, with manes to their knees and tails that dragged behind them!

At the stall door now she looked over the mare with pure pleasure. Then something odd struck her. Turning to Pam she said a little shyly, "That's funny. Have you noticed we each sort of look like our own horse? You and Flight are smaller and dainty, and Challenger and I are what I guess you'd call rugged. And he and I are blonds, just the opposite of you two. You know," she continued on impulse, "when I look at you, I'm sick of my own looks all of a sudden. I wish I had big brown eyes and oodles of bouncy dark hair."

"You could dye your hair," Pam suggested, tossing hers back where it brushed her shoulders. Ellie burst out laughing, imagining Grandpa's shock if she should turn into a brunette.

They compared notes on what classes they had entered here at the fair. Ellie and Challenger were in two before the medal. "So he'll get thoroughly used to the ring with the audience and noise and the loudspeaker," she explained. "He's kind of nervous about people and loud noises. Another thing, I might win some money because one of the classes is Hunter Hacks, with real good prize money."

Pam had entered several classes. "I love to show," she said, "but I don't care much for morning schooling. It means getting up too early. Besides, what's the fun of riding when no one's watching you? Frankly, what I like is being out there alone before a full grandstand, being the star even if it's only for a couple of minutes. It thrills me to pieces to hear applause that's just for me." She spoke so honestly that Ellie couldn't help liking her. Plainly, to Pam the ring was a stage, and she a great actress, playing her part before an adoring public.

The role of groom evidently didn't appeal to Pam, in spite of the fine tools in her trunk. Flight had her own bucket and pan, and a smart red and white blanket, but Pam made no move to feed or water her at feeding time, and ignored the pitchfork. With Grandpa gone to see the blacksmith, Ellie was left to "do up" for the day. The work didn't amount to anything, with only two horses, but it was annoying that Pam sat on a bale of straw watching and didn't offer to help. In silence Ellie haltered Challenger and led him out for a few turns up and down the aisle to stretch his legs. Then she refilled his bucket and gave him his ration of grain and hay. He liked her to be near while he ate, so during his meal she went over his bedding with the pitchfork and removed soiled straw and droppings. Dumping these in the wheelbarrow, she trundled it off to the manure pile at the other end of the aisle.

Back again, she stuck the pitchfork violently into the bale on which Pam sat, missing her by inches.

Pam jumped. "Hey, watch out! You nearly stabbed me."

"I thought you might like to borrow the fork," Ellie said.

Pam turned big reproachful eyes on her. "All right," she answered. "I can take a hint. Show me what to do."

By the time Pam's parents drove up, everything was tidy and both horses were blanketed for the night. It was perhaps as well that Grandpa had not returned, for Pam said casually she would come "about eleven" next morning. In Grandpa's opinion eleven o'clock was practically lunch time, not time to start schooling. However, Ellie didn't dare argue before the Mortons. After all, they were valuable customers.

When they had gone she went to lean on Challenger's door. She loved this time of day when the fairgrounds lay quiet between the day's business and the night's opening of the carnival. The few horsemen who had arrived were off at supper, leaving the aisles empty and silent except for the rhythmic chewing of feeding horses. Above, the sky was just starting to turn pink. Sleepy birds chirped in the palm grove. A distant dog's bark mingled with faint traffic noises. In some other barn a thirsty horse rattled his water bucket; somewhere a nervous one pawed at his door. An hour from now, Ellie knew, the quiet would be shattered by the carnival. Shrieks and clanking machinery, rifle pops and crying kids would make a background racket, though not close. There would be the half sad, half gay music of the merry-go-round which always seemed like the real voice of a fair. If a breeze blew this way Ellie might smell hamburgers and cotton candy and beer. She would see lights against the sky, all shapes and colors, and highest of all, brightest of all, the ferris wheel.

Inside the stall Challenger raised his head from his supper to look at Ellie, plainly inviting her nearer. When she had joined him he turned back satisfied to his hay. For contented minutes she stood beside him, one hand on his withers, which she could just reach. She watched how his lips picked up the hay, then his jaws worked, then he swallowed. At each swallow a kind of wave rippled his throat. From his withers her hand slid forward to finger his mane. The silky chestnut strands

smelled clean from a recent shampoo. His coat, too, smelled clean and healthy. Even the stall smelled good, of rich sweet hay. She ran her hand down his shoulder, feeling the power there. She leaned her head against his side and heard his insides digesting. Against her ear, they sounded like thunder rumbling, and his stomach was warm and furry.

Her hand moved down, sleeking the hair over his foreleg. Bending, she stared at his knee. From a few inches away, knees were weirdly shaped things. Below the knees she admired the white stocking so well matching the other three. Four such even stockings made about the best looking legs a hunter could have, she thought, especially when they were scrubbed snowy white. She licked one finger and rubbed a spot from the near stocking.

Suddenly Challenger raised his head with a mouthful of hay and stopped chewing to listen. The motion lifted his foretop long enough to show the white diamond under it. His deep wise eyes stared off over the half door.

"What's wrong, honey, someone coming?" Ellie asked.

After a moment he gave a relaxed sigh and started chewing again, so she guessed it was Grandpa.

Grandpa held a letter which he had picked up at the

horse show office on the grounds. "From Mr. Sampson," he said. "He can't get here for another few days, but his horse'll be here in the morning. He asks that you show it again in Ladies' and Amateurs', and any other classes he might have to miss."

"Fine," Ellie said. Mr. Sampson's gray gelding, Foam, was like its owner, no thrill but no trouble either. Both were elderly and dependable. Ellie was sure that if Foam could talk he would have the same old-fashioned politeness as Mr. Sampson.

"He'll pay you the usual," Grandpa went on, "which is good and plenty at your age."

Ellie was afraid she might have to hear again how, at her age, Grandpa was earning a shilling, or twenty-five cents a day, walking hots at the Leopardstown track near Dublin, Ireland. "Talking of clients," she said hastily, "when does Billy Bannister arrive?"

"Wednesday, I expect." Grandpa was looking into the stalls, checking on Night Flight and Challenger. Apparently satisfied, he turned back. "Now there's a youngster who'll need a lot of my time. Actually he's too green to be showing, but that's not up to me. I've told his mother so, but the woman never stops talking long enough to listen." Mrs. Bannister, a widow, was tall, toothy and talkative. Supposedly she was husband-hunting and had her eye on Grandpa. "I like Billy,"

he said, "all but his fibbing. To me, dishonest
form is a disgrace. But he does have pluck for .
year-old. He'd be jumping, if that pony of his
too fat to get off the ground. It's not fit. There's a
that fat's a good color, but fit's a mighty good color

As he talked, he and Ellie had started for the tr.
Inside, Grandpa began supper preparations. He hum
"Mother Machree" while he pared potatoes, shel.
peas to the tune of "The Rose of Tralee" and slapp
ground beef patties in time with "When Irish Eyes Ar
Smilin'." Ellie enjoyed the concert while she studied,
stretched on her lower bunk at the other end of the
trailer. She concentrated best when Grandpa was humming, the way some kids turned on the radio to do their
homework. Possibly she would have enjoyed her present
book under any conditions, for it was the American
Horse Shows Association rules. Most of it was real interesting, especially the parts about hunters and jumpers.
She knew many parts by heart, and intended to memo-
rize more. You could never tell what questions a judge
might ask you about conformation, equipment or horsemanship.

"Drill me after supper, Grandpa?" she called during
a pause in his singing.

"I will that," he answered. "As I recall, we need to
review blemishes and unsoundness. Also questions on

appointments. And rules governing certain penalties. Let's see . . . H'm . . . 'When Irish eyes'—Oh yes, we'll run through some definitions too."

Unseen, Ellie lay back with a groan. Might as well say they'd run through the whole darn book!

Not even waiting till after supper, he quizzed her during dessert, ice cream for her, and for him his favorite strong black tea. After an hour's lesson she grew so sleepy that her answers became confused. When she defined a double bridle as "a thing with several reins," Grandpa decided it was bedtime. In her bunk, she wondered how well Pam knew the rule book and how she would like being quizzed by Grandpa. Once during the night she was wakened by the sound of the trailer door opening. She saw a beam from Grandpa's flashlight and heard him step softly out and walk to the stalls. He must be checking on Flight, making sure she had settled down properly her first night here. How careful he always was of the horses in his charge. She was tempted to go see Challenger. It was fun to visit him at night, to see if he was lying down or sleeping upright, to hear him mumble a greeting in the dark. While she struggled to rouse herself, Grandpa's light shone again, the door closed, his bed creaked. She drifted back to sleep under the rustling palm trees.

Next morning was real interesting. Challenger's

schooling came first, then his breakfast, while Grandpa took care of Flight. Their own breakfast came next, interrupted by the arrival of Mr. Sampson's horse trailer. The man hauling it unloaded Foam and left after a cup of coffee. Somehow news got around that the Sayres were serving hot coffee, and several friends and rivals appeared for a cup and stayed to chat. They had come in during the night or early morning with vans, trucks and trailers. Show time seemed suddenly to jump closer.

After breakfast Ellie and her grandfather went to work converting a box stall into a tack room. This had to be done at each show, for with three clients besides themselves there were four sets of tack. Grandpa was more careful of it than if it were all his, and kept it spick and span, with a padlock on the tack-room door. It was fun to fix up the place. First the dirt floor must be swept, and any holes or bumps in it evened. Then a mat was spread as carpeting. Bridle racks were nailed to the walls in neat rows. Wooden saw horses for saddles, one apiece, were placed next to each person's trunk or box.

A horseshoe-shaped mirror was hung, and this always caused a lot of friendly argument. For Grandpa to see himself in it, it should be high. Then little Billy Bannister couldn't use it. If it was low enough for Billy, Ellie had to bend to see her reflection. If it suited Ellie, Mr. Sampson had to bend. In the end it turned out, no one knew just how, that the mirror hung at exactly the best height for Pam.

Last of all, Grandpa drove about a dozen nails at intervals along the walls and hooked clothes hangers over them. Ellie knew by heart the threat that would follow. "Now there's no excuse for people to throw their belongings around. From here on I'll claim anything I pick up." As Grandpa said this, she pictured him picking up and wearing Billy's Mickey Mouse cap, or even her retainer, which was apt to turn up in the weirdest places.

Toward midmorning she was bringing Foam in from exercise when Pam appeared. Pam seemed in no hurry to see Flight. She stopped Ellie to tell what fun she'd had swimming, and all about the motel. "You must come stay with me overnight," she invited.

Ellie noticed again how small Pam's waist was in the jodhpurs, and how her blouse already covered some curves. It was a shame though to let that shiny hair get all dusty in the ring. She offered to lend a bandana, but Pam refused, shaking back her hair in a gesture that showed off its glints and gleams.

At this point their conversation was cut short by Grandpa. "Are you working or playing?" he said to Ellie and to Pam, "Your mare is ready."

Ellie peeked from Foam's stall while she put him away. Grandpa had led Flight out and was giving Pam instructions. She was nodding, smiling up at him while he talked. Then he stepped back and watched her critically as she mounted and took up the reins. As she started out, he said, "I'll look on from the grandstand."

Ellie didn't neglect any part of Foam's routine, but she hurried, and a few minutes later arrived breathless at the ringside. Pam was circling at a walk on the rail, now and then exchanging talk and smiles with the other riders. She was noticing too, Ellie could tell, that quite a few people were sitting idly in the stands, since most had finished their work by this time in the morning. Clearly Pam was pleased to have at least some audience. Also she was pleased that Flight hadn't settled down, but pranced and danced in a manner that attracted attention. Knowing Grandpa so well, Ellie knew he would simply let Flight walk until she did settle down, and until probably Pam grew bored. She saw Pam glance at him several times as if asking for a different gait. Each time he shook his head. It was a full twenty minutes before he allowed her to trot, and another long interval before she might canter.

Pam's seat and hands were good, Ellie saw. She had excellent balance, and her figure was supple, making her a graceful rider. It wasn't possible yet to guess how much nerve or strength or judgment she would have. Ellie could see various small faults which she was sure

Grandpa hadn't missed. One was that Pam's feet weren't quite deep enough into the stirrups. One was that she held her elbows a little too far from her body. These faults could probably be corrected easily. Pam's main fault was more serious: her mind was not on her work.

Finally Grandpa rose in the stands, and Ellie entered the ring to help him set up jumps. Pam met the two of them in the center. "Well, at last!" she exclaimed. "I was beginning to think I'd never get to jump today." She glanced at the few remaining onlookers as if she feared they too might drift off.

"You were thinking right," Grandpa said.

"What!" Both girls spoke at once. Grandpa looked at Ellie. "You can go now. I won't need your help." One thing he wouldn't stand for was interference during a lesson. Why hadn't she kept quiet!

She walked to the ring gate as slowly as possible. From there she couldn't hear much of what Grandpa was saying. Mostly, she did catch, he told Pam that neither she nor her mare was ready to jump. Pam argued, but he interrupted. "You weren't paying attention. Until you do, there'll be no jumping." He went on talking, and now Pam didn't answer at all. She just sat, looking sulky.

All three returned in silence to the barn. Pam slid off her mare, evidently meaning simply to walk away and leave her. Ellie had to catch Flight. She didn't want things to get worse. "I'll cool her and put her away if you have to go," she said to Pam. She knew Pam had walked from the motel, which was close to the grounds.

"Just a minute." Grandpa spoke directly to Pam. "If you expect to improve, we'd better have another schooling this afternoon. Say three o'clock?"

"No thanks," Pam muttered. Her face wasn't pretty now, but defiant.

There was silence. Ellie felt the tug of reins in her hand. Challenger called her, but she stood as if rooted.

"I'll expect you at three," Grandpa said evenly to Pam.

"No."

"No?" Frosty blue eyes met stubborn brown ones, and neither yielded.

With a visible effort Grandpa remained cool. "What reason have you against schooling again?"

Pam replied with a shrug that was pure temper.

"In that case," he concluded, "you'd better find another trainer."

Pam turned and left without answering.

It was so quiet at Barn B that Ellie could clearly hear the traffic in town. She glanced at Grandpa, and he motioned her to put Flight away. While she was unsaddling she heard him go into the trailer.

Lunch was ready when she joined him. It was nearly

one, but she wasn't hungry. He didn't eat much either, but sat stirring his black tea. The lines in his face were deeper than usual and for once his shoulders sagged. It was a grim meal. Neither wanted to talk just for talking's sake. He too was thinking, Ellie guessed, that Pam was the first pupil he had lost. It was going to cost him, not only in money but in reputation. Already she could hear rival trainers saying that Patrick Sayre had been fool enough to lose his best customer. They would use the fact as proof that now definitely he was too old for the job.

Ellie felt a rush of love for him. He was old . . . but not too old to stand up for his rights. Pride mingled with her love. She knew how much he needed what the Mortons would have paid him, and she admired him with all her heart for risking its loss since he felt that was the right course. She admired him all the more when he said briskly, "We'll wait until three o'clock before getting in touch with Mr. Morton. Meantime I'll have a look at the paper, and you'd better go on with that mending you started." As if this was any ordinary afternoon!

On her bunk, Ellie found she couldn't concentrate. She kept picturing Grandpa's tired face, and Pam's sullen one. Poor silly Pam. Had she told her parents what she'd done? They must be furious. Or maybe she hadn't yet had the nerve to tell them. Probably by now she would give anything to unsay her words. Well, all she had to do was show up at three o'clock. Only she wouldn't. She'd be too proud. If there were just some way to make coming back less embarrassing! Ellie remembered times when she herself had been dying for an excuse to make up . . . Well, then, why didn't she help Pam, and at the same time help Grandpa? He was proud too. He wasn't going to change his mind, she was positive of that. So why was she just sitting here, doing nothing?

"What's the matter with me!" she exclaimed, jumping up. "But take it easy," she warned herself. "You've got to be real foxy about this."

She strolled into Grandpa's room and opened the trailer door with some excuse of going out for air. Her watch said two thirty. She made herself walk as far as she figured Grandpa could hear her, then broke into a mad run. Past the ring she raced, past the horse show office, past an astonished Rolly, who yelled, "Where's the fire?" She tore through the silent carnival area and reached the street beyond. Her hair was standing up and her retainer was dry from panting. Sweat dripped inside her shirt, but nothing slowed her up. Only one block now to the motel. At a desperate pace she dodged an old lady, bumped a man and jumped a dog. At last, the Date Tree!

Five minutes later she was headed back to the fairgrounds, but at a slower pace because she was dragging Pam by the hand. It really hadn't been hard to persuade Pam to come. Ellie had simply overwhelmed her with words, much in the style of Mrs. Bannister. Now Pam was putting on a great show of protesting and hanging back. "But I'm not sorry," she said for the third time. "I'm not ashamed."

"Of course you're not," Ellie soothed her, knowing Pam had to have an excuse to apologize. "All you have to do is pretend," she urged, hurrying along. "Just act. *Act*, see?"

By the time they passed the ring she felt it was safe to drop back. She was too worn out to hurry any more. Besides, she musn't show up at the trailer with Pam, or breathless and limp. As Pam ran ahead, Ellie followed slowly, tucking her shirt into her jeans and combing back her bangs with her fingers. When she reached the trailer at three minutes to three, she regretted that she had missed the act. It must have been good.

"Very well then, let's get to work," Grandpa was saying.

There was something very real in the way Pam answered. "Yes, and—I'm sorry." If Pam hadn't meant that, she couldn't have sounded so convincing. She wasn't that good an actress, Ellie thought with satisfaction.

3. Sentenced to Hard Labor

THE days that followed seemed to Ellie each one busier than the last. From the moment the sun first flickered through the palm trees until it sank behind the carnival, all parts of the day were filled with excitement and interest. There was work too, naturally, which made Pam grumble, "This is worse than being sentenced to hard labor."

In spite of frequent complaints Pam was improving, not only in horsemanship but in attitude. After that one revolt against Grandpa, she hadn't dared cross him again. Not that she didn't often get her way. She got it, Ellie realized, by acting so sweet that people couldn't resist her.

Ellie liked Pam more and more, in spite of the fact that she saw through her. They were fast becoming real friends. Each learned about the other's life. They discussed home, school and parents. They agreed that boys were worms, and then agreed, giggling, that some worms could be awfully cute. Ellie told how she was collecting stuffed animals at home; Pam was collecting costume dolls. They were very frank about each other's looks. Pam was going to be the glamorous type and go in for romances and of course for a career in the movies. Ellie would some day look terribly smart and sporty in expensive suits. She would become a famous trainer like Grandpa. Both girls might or might not get married, but if they did they were determined not to be problems to their children. Above all they agreed it was lucky they had met, and this was going to be a wonderful summer.

Some of their conversations were held in Ellie's "room," where they had to be careful because of Grandpa, for the room had no door. The opening into the passage between bathroom and closets could be screened only by a curtain. They pulled it when Pam settled on the lower bunk to talk while Ellie sewed, cleaned shoes or ironed. Still, since the passage led into Grandpa's room, he could hear them if he was home. There was much whispering and smothered laughter, which made visiting all the more fun. More risky too, at times, such as the afternoon Pam produced the cigarettes. She had taken them from her father's case. "There's no reason we shouldn't try smoking," she said daringly.

Ellie was horrified on Grandpa's account. "If he finds out he'll murder me," she whispered. But she couldn't refuse for fear Pam would think her cowardly.

They peeked from the windows to make sure Grandpa wasn't around, then pulled the curtain across the opening to Ellie's room. Pam lit her cigarette as casually as if it wasn't her first. Ellie's fingers shook so that she burned them and wasted five matches. The cigarette tasted horrible. Pam laughed at her, and then she started laughing, because in spite of her casual air Pam was smoking the wrong end. Between laughing and coughing they shook so hard that the bed shook.

"Look at yourself!" Ellie gasped. "You're turning purple."

"You should talk!" Pam retorted. "You're green. And your eyes are bulging. You look like a frog."

"Stop," Ellie moaned, doubling up. "I'm dying. Oh, my stomach!"

"I'm sick," Pam said, puffing and choking. Both grew hysterical and the experiment ended when, half-strangled, Ellie coughed out her retainer.

These periods of nonsense were rare for Ellie. Besides housework and Challenger, she helped care for Flight and did all the exercising of Foam. She had more and more outside jobs as more horses arrived on the grounds. There was always someone who wanted a horse walked or led, or held for washing, trimming or shoeing. Others needed help fixing their tack rooms. Still others had errands to be run, from mailing letters at the street corner or buying the daily paper there, to sewing a button on a shirt or coat. Everybody knew Ellie and counted on her efficiency. She was glad nobody seemed to notice how easily she could forget! Her earnings grew by small but steady sums. The only person for whom she wouldn't work was the trainer Bull Johnson. It upset her even to be near him, to hear his swearing and shouting, and to see the nervous condition of his jumpers. Several times she had watched them win, but she hated to think what kind of schooling they had been through to do it. It was no wonder they were skinny.

On the Wednesday before opening day of the show the Bannisters arrived. Mrs. Bannister was driving, hauling the fat pony who went by the splendid and inappropriate name of King of the Plains. While Mrs. Bannister engulfed Grandpa in a torrent of words, Ellie escaped by leading King to his stall, followed by Billy. To please him she remarked that King was looking real well.

"Sure he is," Billy answered. "He looks so good a man wanted to buy him. He said he'd pay five thousand dollars for him."

"Oh Billy, no. That's impossible."

As usual Billy stuck to his story, gazing up from clear blue eyes innocent as an angel's. His fair curly hair and round face added to the angelic impression no matter what absurd lies he invented.

The first one he told Pam brought a scolding from her. "You better be nice to me," he retorted, "or my mother will send you to jail. She's not wearing her uniform here, so I guess you didn't know she's a sheriff."

Pam jeered in disbelief. "You're a little monster," she said. This Billy took as a compliment, and at once fell in love with her. He told Ellie with exasperating nerve that he and Pam were engaged.

Ellie wished Pam would take riding more seriously. Maybe it wasn't her nature to be truly serious about anything. She enjoyed riding, particularly in company, and she was paying more attention to Grandpa and less to other onlookers. And she was working to correct her feet and elbows. But she grew discouraged or impatient so easily. Her chances of winning a medal were only fair, with more competitors arriving each day. Especially, Ellie realized, with herself and Challenger to beat. Without them, Pam's chances would be much better. Of course it would be fine for Grandpa if either of them won. But there were moments when Ellie wished she wasn't competing against Pam. There were even moments when she wondered if, in the class, she ought not to ride less well than she could. If she won here, though, at the next show in Santa Barbara she could concentrate on helping Pam, since she herself wouldn't be trying for a medal. Once you had your medal, you stayed out till the finals. If this plan worked, Grandpa would have two winners in one season, which would make him real proud. It would be specially good because they were both young to ride against contestants up to eighteen years old.

It wasn't only Grandpa and herself that Ellie wanted to please by winning her medal. She was sure Challenger too would be proud, that he understood about winning. At least in the ring he knew what to do. He helped her.

At some early stage of his career he must have had proper training. It showed in his style of jumping, in the way he went at his fences, in his timing. Too, his size and good build made possible his long stride, easy gallop and powerful spring. Ellie felt there were only two points on which he could be faulted. He took quite a hold at times; and he might be considered a little big for a child's mount. As to his disposition, he was settling day by day, growing farther from the nervous wreck he had been. For instance, he wasn't a bit suspicious of Pam. Nothing, Ellie resolved, must happen to upset all this. Nothing must ever turn him back into the pitiful creature she had first known. As Grandpa said, "He has a proud name. Let's see that he lives up to it."

If Ellie's days were full, Grandpa's were fuller. He supervised every horse's exercise, different in each case. He watched just what each ate and drank, occasionally varying their diets. Separately he coached Ellie, Pam, and Billy. He drilled both girls with books and charts, and showed Billy the simpler ones, with an eye to the future. Often he was called by other stables for advice. And almost jealously he took entire care of the tack. For this he had his own box of special soaps, creams, oil and polish which he used in a secret routine, humming mournfully as he worked. His best tune was an absolute heartbreaker called "Farewell, Shamrock Shores." For some weird reason he hummed it only when things were going specially well. Like a good cook unwilling to give out precious recipes, he dodged questions about just how he cleaned leather and steel so beautifully.

"Oh, a lick o' this and a lick o' that," he would say. "Mainly an old-fashioned item called elbow grease."

When the carnival had first opened he had ignored Ellie's nightly gaze toward the bright lights. He had pretended not to notice how the glow of them tempted her, along with the noise of voices and music, the smells, the loot brought back by friends, above all the sight of the ferris wheel turning like a great jeweled ring in the sky.

But he couldn't hold out forever. Because of the carnival there would be no night horse show, and once the daily shows started he would insist on early bedtimes. On Thursday, two days before the show, he told Ellie to go ahead and get it over. Joyfully she and Pam agreed to meet after supper and tour the carnival.

"But no lingering late," he warned Ellie, "and no talking to strangers. Another thing, Pamela may have plenty of money to spend, but I'd advise you not to throw yours away on a lot of junk. Not that you haven't earned it," he added, "though at your age I worked much harder for—"

"I know, a shilling a day walking hots at the Leopardstown track," Ellie said quickly. Just as quickly she realized it was mean to act impatient when he spoke of what small pay he used to earn. If work could make a man rich, he should be a millionaire. But in the horse business no one got rich. She knew he hadn't saved much for the time when old age would force him to retire.

That evening, behind her curtain, she changed into her dress. With only one dress in the trailer she would have liked to keep it fresh for church on Sunday. But Pam had coaxed, "Oh, let's look nice for once. I'm sick of pants. Let's doll up."

Their plan had almost been wrecked that afternoon when Billy disovered it and begged to be included. They didn't object to taking him, but they did object to having Mrs. Bannister along. Pam suggested innocently to Grandpa that he date Billy's mother to keep her out of the way, a suggestion he rejected with panic. In the end the girls compromised by promising to take Billy some other time.

"If there's anything left of us," Pam groaned, "after all this schooling. Honestly, I'm a wreck. Every bone aches. I'd like never again to hear those words of your grandfather's, 'Are you working or playing?' "

She looked anything but a wreck when Ellie met her at the Date Tree that evening. Her parents had already left for dinner in Palm Springs, a few miles away. They had friends there with whom they spent most of their time so that, as Pam said, they weren't giving her any trouble. However, they had told her to be back early tonight. "But they didn't mention how early," she said slyly. Her brown eyes danced with mischief, matching the saucy bounce of the hair on her shoulders. Her dress was red linen, with a lower neck line than Ellie would have worn. The high-heeled sandals and costume jewelry, it seemed, were Mrs. Morton's. Ellie suspected Mrs. Morton didn't know she had lent them, or that her daughter was wearing lipstick, nail polish and perfume.

By comparison Ellie thought she herself looked awfully young in her blue cotton print. She had chosen it last year because it was a drip-dry and wouldn't need ironing. Now she was outgrowing it, which made it seem all the more babyish, along with her flats and no make-up. But then she wasn't playing a part, while Pam was trying to be a sophisticated young lady.

Five minutes after meeting they entered the carnival, and it was as exciting as always. Slowly they pushed their way along, holding hands so as not to be swept apart by the crowds. They wandered from booth to booth, half-dazed by the lights and the racket. Loud noises pierced the hum of voices, and strange smells pierced the background smell of food and people. Everywhere kids dodged about, yelling, their faces smeared with cotton candy. Older folks drifted on the moving current. Here and there a couple of lovers walked with arms linked, or just stood and gazed at each other while the lights colored their faces pink, then blue, then orange.

Ellie wasted a few dimes throwing rings and balls at targets. She wanted to win another stuffed animal for her collection. Pam tried too and won a tiger, which she gave to Ellie. They rode the Bumper Bumps, metal cars that crashed into one another with deafening bangs.

They cruised in a boat, the passengers shrieking and giggling through the dark tunnels. They mounted gorgeous steeds on the merry-go-round. They stared with fascination at the Wild Man, who was really kind of a pitiful old guy. And all this time they progressed as if drawn by a magnet toward the loudest, brightest and dizziest of all rides, the ferris wheel.

At last they were seated together in it, behind a safety bar. Waiting to be airborne, they heard their names called from in back. Turning, Pam reported, "It's the Andrews twins, some of our medal class competition."

Ellie took one hand from her tiger to wave hello. Under the noise of starting she said, "They're real nice, but not terribly good riders. At least, they ride better Western. Almost no one can be tops in both." It struck her that most of the top riders she knew weren't here. They must be at some other show which was holding a medal class too. Then for once she forgot horses and riders in the thrill of the moment.

Slowly they swung out and up, widening the drop to earth. By jolts and jars they rose, while the world below dwindled into a tiny map. When they had the nerve to look, they saw the whole carnival area spread beneath them. Beyond, they picked out the dark ring, the rows of barns, and farther still the black mass of the palm grove. Off to one side the lights of Palm Springs twinkled. Nearer again, Ellie tried to find the trailer but couldn't, mostly because she couldn't bear to look down. With Pam she shared a sort of delightful terror that made them clutch each other and scream like lunatics.

It seemed ages later they returned to earth and staggered from their seats. Sid and Sue Andrews joined them, to talk horse while they strolled. The twins and Pam hoped to do some winning this weekend, when the classes would be open only to children. From Monday on, competition would be tougher. Ellie hadn't entered the children's classes because Grandpa felt that with her knowledge and experience she was well ahead of the others. It wouldn't look good to have her beating too many clients in too many classes.

Sid pretended to feel the deepest sympathy for Pam, obliged to compete against her "stable mate" Ellie for the medal. "Poor girl, she hasn't a chance," he said.

"We haven't either, let's face it," Sue said cheerfully. "Ellie's bound to win."

"Thanks, but far from it," Ellie protested. "You know perfectly well anybody can win."

"Who, for instance?" Sid asked, and Ellie was startled that she couldn't honestly name anyone more likely than herself. "Maybe Pete Dokes, from Bakersfield," she suggested.

Of the four, Pam seemed to care least. "Oh well, what does it matter anyway?" she said, a question Ellie found upsetting.

"Even if I should happen to win here," she told Pam, "you'll try again at Santa Barbara or other places."

"Or give up," said Pam, which was more than upsetting. It was shocking. Why, if Pam quit, they might never see each other again, with Pam living in Los Angeles and Ellie in South San Francisco.

Because of Pam's attitude, a feeling of depression began to creep over Ellie. For her, the fun went out of the evening. She strolled about with the others, but she scarcely heard their jokes and teasing, and didn't join in their laughter. Quite early she gave some excuse about having to get back to the trailer. She wanted to be alone, to think out this question of Pam and the medal. After she made sure the twins would see Pam safely to the Date Tree, she turned her back on the evening's gaiety and headed for the barns. From glare into gloom she walked slowly, deep in thought. By the time she reached the trailer she had faced the truth that if Pam didn't win it would be because of her. With her help, Pam might win. She could make her win!

Grandpa's light was on. She knew he was waiting for her, but somehow she wasn't ready to talk to him yet. "I'm back," she called. "I'll be in soon." Knowing her habits, he could guess where she would be.

A nicker greeted her as she opened the stall door. By starlight and the carnival's glow she could make out that Challenger was lying down. Speaking softly, she stepped over the silvery patches of his white stockings and settled in the straw beside him. A year ago he

wouldn't have allowed this. In those days he would cringe into the farthest corner when anyone entered his stall.

"It's different now, isn't it, honey?" she said, reaching gently to smooth his neck. "Look, I brought you a mascot."

Dimly she saw his head raise and turn toward her. He nuzzled the tiger in acceptance. She lifted his foretop to rub his fine brow, and the white diamond there gleamed faintly. His eyes were deep and trusting. They made her wish she could forget the plan forming in her mind . . . But Pam needed to win. Pam had hinted that if she didn't win she would give up. Then what? She would go back to being just another silly movie-mad girl. Ellie would lose a new friend, and Grandpa a valuable pupil. He would be cruelly disappointed, both for his reputation and his savings.

"It's different for me," she said in the dark. "If I don't win here, I'll most likely win somewhere else." Her voice wasn't steady, and her heart felt unsteady too. It was heavy with sadness, not so much for herself as for someone who maybe needed to win as much as Pam did. Horses as well as people wanted to prove how well they had learned, after months and months of trying. Wouldn't a horse feel bitter at having to lose? She knew the answer where Challenger was concerned. When he won, he carried himself proud as a champion. When he lost, something went out of him, like part of his heart.

Ellie leaned forward. For a long time she stared at her horse, following his thoughts, hoping he couldn't guess hers.

4. A Dirty Trick

THE day before the show opened was so busy that Ellie scarcely had time to think over her plan to ride badly in the medal class. Luckily the class wasn't due for another nine days. It was scheduled for the last Saturday of the show. Surely in nine days she would be able to figure a way to lose which would fool even Grandpa. The simplest way would be to scratch, but that would mean embarrassing explanations. Of course it was just possible Pam would improve so much, or her attitude would change so much, that this miserable scheme wouldn't be necessary.

This Friday began badly for Ellie when she realized that once again her old devil forgetfulness had won a point. She had left her tiger in Challenger's stall the night before. He must have used it for chewing gum, for this morning it was mashed to rags. Sadly she threw it into the wheelbarrow when she cleaned the stall.

Then Pam turned up late, having overslept. Next, King of the Plains dumped Billy, for which Billy called him a dumb old donkey. Foam developed a cough. And, to Grandpa's embarrassment, Mrs. Bannister brought her knitting—socks, which she announced she was making for him. Yet in a gloomy way the succession of mishaps pleased him. It was one of his sayings that things couldn't always go right, therefore it was best to have your troubles before rather than during the show. Still he wasn't disappointed when Challenger put on an excellent performance.

Ellie was schooling for the hunter hack class next Monday. In that class a loose rein would be required, which was asking a lot of Challenger because he liked to take hold. This morning, for some reason, he held a steady pace without pulling. She thought it might be because every single day he was listening a little more obediently to her voice. Or, as the saying went, to her hands. At any rate, his long stride outwalked and out-trotted most horses in the ring, and his canter on a slack rein was a dream of style and ease. Ellie and Grandpa didn't have him jump, so that in the class he would concentrate on his rail work instead of looking for fences. After such a good go, it was no wonder Grandpa hummed "Farewell Shamrock Shores," a sure sign he was pleased.

"I hope Challenger's still in this mood Monday," Ellie told Pam. "With two days of children's show coming up we're all liable to be out of our minds by then. One good thing though, we'll get Billy's classes all over during the weekend."

"But Mrs. Bannister'll make some excuse to stay on so she can flirt with your Grandpa," Pam said.

Ellie laughed. "Oh, sure. The excuse is having Billy take lessons the rest of the week. Hey, an idea. Maybe she'd like to do some of my housework. That way she could impress Grandpa."

"I'd as soon not be riding till Monday myself," Pam remarked. "But my equitation class is tomorrow, the fourteen and under. Still, I'll probably have a good chance in it since you're not entered, thank heavens."

"Of course you'll have a good chance," Ellie said warmly. "Just never mind who's entered or who isn't, and especially never mind the audience. Go in there fighting."

"Make me mad then, just before the class," Pam giggled.

Ellie gazed reflectively at her friend's pretty face

and decided that was exactly what she would do—make Pam mad just before her class. It was worth a try, to stir up her fighting spirit.

By Saturday noon the show grounds were jammed with what seemed thousands of children. From toddlers to eighteen-year-olds, they were everywhere on every type of mount, both English and Western. All pedestrians were in danger of being bumped, kicked or trampled. Parents too came in mobs, each interested solely in his own little darling. Ellie was thankful the Mortons weren't the anxious kind who might upset their daughter. They didn't fuss when they arrived with Pam's show clothes and a gorgeous chicken and salad picnic. They had guessed that today there would be less time than usual for cooking at the trailer. Besides, they claimed to owe the Sayres several meals because lately Pam had taken to eating lunch with Ellie.

"I'm happy to see the child eat well," Grandpa told Mrs. Morton. His lined face was serious as he went on. "Being in this business year after year, I've learned not to skip meals or sleep. Youngsters are apt to think they're too nervous to eat before a class, and if encouraged that can grow into a dangerous habit. A certain amount of tension may be natural, but generally I ignore their nerves and—" he twinkled—"their stomachs."

A Dirty Trick

At length, after appropriate ceremonies, the show opened with a lead-line class. Ten young hopefuls and their guides rode in with dignity which soon turned to confusion. There was one runaway, luckily only trotting; one horse balked; several pairs separated. Hats, whips and numbers went flying. One jockey fell off, one got the giggles, one wept. Two pairs became tangled and ended as a foursome. Altogether the class was hilarious for the audience.

At three o'clock Billy showed in a class in which the mounts were judged on suitability to rider. Unfortunately he rode with more daring than skill. He urged King along so fast that they kept passing everyone else. The poor fat beast gave a false impression that he was bolting. They left the ring with no award, to be met by Grandpa. "Next time, Billy," he said sternly, "remember your riding lessons. Otherwise we're wasting our time and your mother's money."

To Ellie's dismay, Grandpa told her to see Billy safely back to Barn B just as Pam's equitation class was being called. She knew better than to argue, but she wasn't going to give up making Pam mad. With a hand on King's bridle she stopped by Pam, who was waiting at the gate with the rest of the class.

"I bet you'll do worse than Billy," Ellie said nastily,

low enough so that only Pam could hear. "You can't even act like a good rider. You can't act at all, I bet, and you never will!"

She heard Pam's indignant "Well!" as the class filed in. Pam's chin was up, her shoulders were squared. Even her back bristled with determination. Leading King to the barn, Ellie wondered if she had made a horrible mistake by insulting Pam. If she had dared trust Billy to cool King properly she would have run back to the ring.

It was Billy who ran off and Ellie who still walked the pony when Pam galloped back fifteen minutes later. There was fire in her eyes and—a blue ribbon in her hand!

"Ellen Sayre . . ." she exploded, her face pink with anger. And there she stopped. She stared at Ellie, who was laughing, rushing over to pat Pam's leg, her mare, anything within reach. All at once Pam understood. She too began to laugh, and she jumped off to hug Ellie, exclaiming, "Oh thanks! It worked! Thanks!" Ellie hugged back. "Congratulations, Pam, congratulations! If only I could have watched you," she ended with a wail.

"Frankly, I must have been sensational," Pam boasted, "because Grandpa said I did a pretty fair job."

"If he said that, you were sensational!" Ellie chuckled.

"Madison Square Garden, here I come," Pam said, which caused Ellie a stab of envy.

They had to cut short their chatter because Billy had another class. This time he rode better and was delighted to receive a pink ribbon, fifth award.

Pam won nothing in her second class, for the amazing reason that she missed it. Ellie was bewildered, Grandpa indignant. Only Pam appeared unruffled, when she arrived at the ring too late. She had been off gossiping with Sid and Sue Andrews and hadn't heard the loudspeaker call the class. Shrugging, she tossed off the matter with her favorite expression, "Oh well." Ellie told her crossly she was impossible.

Next day, Sunday, Ellie was up even earlier than usual to finish her chores and housework before she dressed for church. Behind the curtain of her room she changed into her blue dress. She tied on a bandana and pushed her spiky bangs under it. At the bathroom mirror she inspected her face for new freckles and was pleased not to find any. She gave her retainer an extra good scrub and her fingernails a special cleaning. It was funny how you forgot boring things like nails no matter how old you grew.

Grandpa too was wearing his good clothes, an ancient suit which disguised his bowlegs, a dark tie, black shoes, and a hat in place of his cap. He had grudgingly agreed to let the Bannisters pick up him and Ellie. As he told Ellie, "Billy and his mother should be at their best in church, because it is the one place where Billy can't talk nonsense and Mrs. Bannister can't talk at all."

Ellie tried to keep her mind on the service, but it strayed constantly to the show. In the middle of the sermon she found herself recalling Pam's equitation class. The fact that Pam had won it proved the judge liked her horsemanship. That was a good sign for the medal class, in which she would meet much the same competition. Still, Ellie knew she was a better rider than Pam and than most of the others. She should be. Also, she felt she could rely on Challenger more than Pam could on Flight. There wasn't nearly as strong a bond between those two. Yes, she would beat Pam in the medal class . . . if she tried.

She knelt to join in the prayer, then stood to sing with the rest. Again her mind wandered, this time to a picture of Challenger as she had seen him this morning. He had been at his stall door, staring down the aisle toward the ring. Something over there had caught his attention, so that he stood motionless as a great statue horse, eyes fixed, ears and nostrils intent. He looked absolutely— well, noble, she had thought. It was the only word for him. Posing like that, he had reminded her of Grandpa's words: "He has a proud name. Let's see that he lives up to it." Now half-aware of the hymn, Ellie wished she could forget those words. They made her uncomfortable. It was almost as if she meant to disgrace Challenger's proud name in the medal class.

"Please make him not care," she prayed. "You'll have him understand, won't You?"

Back at the trailer by ten o'clock she hurriedly changed again. Grandpa wanted to attend personally to Foam's exercise because the gray was still coughing a little. He shouldn't be ridden, only led by Grandpa, who would listen to his breathing and watch him for signs of sickness. This gave Ellie an interval to help some friends, younger kids who would be showing this afternoon. They hadn't yet learned properly to braid their hunters and couldn't afford to pay anyone to do it. She was teaching them, meanwhile braiding their horses for free. Show people should help each other, she figured. Most of them did the swellest things for a rival who happened to be hurt, broke, or in other trouble.

She found her friends waiting for her at Barn E. There were three of them, all fussing over their horses and talking at once. Like many amateurs, they were nervous about showing, with that scariness Ellie recognized as half fun and half misery.

Setting down her stool, she checked her pockets to make sure she had brought all her tools: comb and scissors, wire and thread. Then she climbed the stool at the first horse's shoulder, handed her dandy brush to the horse's owner and went to work fast. "This isn't going to be a professional job," she warned the kids. "You know it takes me at least an hour to do a full mane and tail. But we'll do the best we can. Watch now, so you'll learn. And if you don't mind, shut up, won't you?"

She moved quickly, smoothing down the mane with the damp brush, then parting it into small sections for braids. She combed each section, braided it, then tied stout brown thread around the end. She doubled the braid under and with her length of bent wire pulled the thread through at the base of the mane, tied and cut it. Then she made the next braid and the next, fingers flying. The kids kept glancing toward the ring and exchanging worried signals as the loudspeaker began to tune up. Already some riders for the first class were mounting. Parents were starting their warnings, threats and don't-forgets. Ellie could see that she wasn't going to complete eleven to thirteen braids per horse. She decided to finish most of each mane, let the youngsters continue on their own, and skip tails. Grandpa would be expecting her to help him with Pam and Billy, and she was careful always to show him how useful she could be so that some day he would take her as his assistant.

That afternoon held the usual fun and commotion of any children's show. There was a hint of tragedy too in a bad spill. Ellie shivered as the long gray ambulance wailed its way into the ring. With other onlookers she cheered when the injured boy was able to wave from his stretcher before he disappeared.

Monday morning a different atmosphere spread through the show grounds as adults took over in place of children. It was no longer simply a question of fun. These people's living depended on the cash prizes they won. Of course there were still some youngsters, and women riders who were a bit forbidding. At this early hour most of them wore jeans, with a shirt or sweater and any old shoes and sweat-stained gloves and no make-up. Bandanas bulged over bobby pins and metal curlers. It was hard to believe these were the same women who later would appear in smart English or Western outfits, or all dressed up to drive hackneys or Shetlands or fine harness horses.

All this Ellie took in absently while she guided Challenger around the crowded ring. Again he went well. He didn't even get panicky when a crazy jumper landed almost on top of him. She felt good when Grandpa said, "That'll do." Challenger felt good too. She could tell by the proud way he walked out, with arched neck, looking around much as Pam did for applause.

Next she rode Foam, but not for long. His cough had gone, so he should be all right for the ladies' class to-morrow. Luckily he was an experienced campaigner who needed no schooling. "I bet he'd go his same old steady way if I showed him with my eyes shut," Ellie told Grandpa.

"That's a foolish attitude," Grandpa said sharply. He stood a moment with a kind of inward look as if he was thinking way back to the past. Then he went on. "Sometime I'll tell you about a jockey who lost a rich race because he was too confident of winning."

"Was it you?" Ellie guessed. "Oh, Grandpa, tell me now!"

He shook his head. "Later. Right now we're working, not playing. You have some braiding to do, and I have tack to clean."

At noon Ellie laid out her clothes for the hunter hack class. She brushed her checked jacket and jodhpurs, polished her jodhpur boots, ironed a tie and brought her white shirt from the closet. Then she reached under her bunk for the box containing her hunting cap. She smoothed the cap lovingly, running her fingers over its velvety texture. She would have liked Pam to see her in this outfit, but Pam was taking the day off. Surprisingly, Grandpa hadn't objected. "I've learned not to ask too much of certain people," he had explained to Ellie. "Pamela may do her best riding, or best anything, when she isn't pushed."

Pam did her best when she was mad, Ellie said to

herself. Only that wouldn't work twice because Pam would recognize the trick.

Grandpa was going on. "Other individuals, you may have noticed, need to be somewhat bullied into performing. And still others can't perform unless they feel your support backing them up." Like Challenger, Ellie thought.

A little before two o'clock she approached the warm-up area on Challenger. Circling there with the other riders, she could see into the ring, where the lightweight stock-horse class was in progress. Out here the footing was grass, and there was no dust. She was glad of this, for she had washed Challenger's white stockings till they practically glistened. She noticed with pride how people who were watching the warming up watched Challenger most of all. They paid him such compliments as, "That handsome big horse," and "Now there's a real hunter hack," and more. Certainly she should place in this class, maybe even win. Her toughest competition would be a good-looking bay belonging to Bull Johnson and ridden by a friend of his.

"It's about time to trot," she said, seeing that half the stock horses had worked. One of them must have been extra good, for a sudden burst of applause startled Challenger. She took him to the end of the warm-up place farthest from the stands, wanting him calm so that he would go quietly on a loose rein. "Relax, honey," she said. "Grandpa'll come from the barn as soon as he's through talking business there. I'll check the girth, then we'll have a nice easy trot. All right?"

Pulling up in a deserted corner, she leaned to feel her girth. The next second she nearly fell off. Challenger had jumped violently and now stood tense, snorting under his breath. Straightening, Ellie saw why. Behind her, a hunting whip had been cracked by an onlooker she hadn't noticed. He was a heavy man with a loose sloppy face—Bull Johnson. He seemed to be just playing with the whip, for his own horse was nowhere near. He appeared not even to have seen Ellie, and now he was idly rolling up his whip's lash. She moved away hurriedly, but as Challenger stepped off, the lash flicked again behind him and cut the air with a zing.

The whole thing had been acted so casually and so fast that not much harm should have been done, but it was enough to upset Challenger. He was halfway across the grass before Ellie could pull him up. She actually felt his heart beating in big thumps between her legs. Within a minute sweat broke out on his neck. He ignored her voice and soothing hands as if they were a stranger's. Desperately she repeated, "Go in there fighting," but for once it didn't help. Even before sidling into the ring instead of walking flat-footed, she knew that she hadn't

a chance. Challenger was unsettled at all gaits, and plainly had his mind on one thing only—that whip. She caught a glimpse of Grandpa near the gate, his face bewildered. After what seemed endless vain struggles, she had to watch Bull Johnson's horse take first place.

At the barn, Grandpa listened to her story in grim silence. Then all he said was, "Let me think this over. You'd better stay on Challenger and walk him till he's quiet, if it takes all evening."

Later that afternoon they talked over the incident. Ellie was close to tears, and all for protesting to the manager, the other exhibitors, everybody.

"Protest what?" Grandpa said. "No one but you saw or paid attention to Johnson. Naturally he would deny upsetting your horse, or he would say it was accidental. There are some who might accuse us of making up excuses because we hadn't won. We would be called poor sports." He held up a hand to keep her from interrupting and finished quite severely. "Another thing, Ellen. Johnson knows that I didn't see this happen. If I should complain, it's perfectly possible he'll make more trouble for you. So I forbid you to repeat the story to anyone."

"Not even to Pam?"

"Right." Grandpa looked old and tired. Ellie could imagine how much he hated to accept defeat. And besides the harm to Challenger, they had wasted an entry fee and missed winning a check.

"A dirty trick," he was muttering. "A dirty dishonest trick, and you know what I think of dishonesty." Oh yes, she had heard him say that dishonesty in any form was a disgrace.

In bed that night under the whispering palms, she discovered that she was too tired to sleep. It had taken ages to quiet Challenger, for he wouldn't relax until she had relaxed herself. Then he had taken more ages over his supper, not really eating but just pushing the hay around and nibbling at the grain. He acted ashamed because he had lost a class which he could have won.

Now she brooded over what had happened, and over Challenger and the medal class. Her conscience lingered uneasily over the medal class. Things people had said kept chasing around in her brain. First Pam's hint about quitting, her careless "Oh well." Then her own decision to lose the class—in a way, to cheat. Then Grandpa's repeated warning that dishonesty in any form was a disgrace. Saying her prayers didn't help. She had the dreadfulest feeling that God disapproved of her, that He wouldn't make Challenger understand about losing the medal.

5. Mental Class Maniacs

ANYBODY could get used to anything, Ellie decided a few days later. It was the middle of the week and now she had accepted the idea of not trying to win the medal class. She didn't let herself think about it. She worked harder than ever and coached Pam so eagerly Pam complained. "You're getting as strict as Grandpa. I can feel a nervous breakdown coming on." These complaints worried Ellie. Maybe she was pushing Pam too hard; yet Ellie gloated over the results of her help. Pam's seat was steadily improving, and also her knowledge of rules and charts and questions. She had a quick mind and a memory that Ellie envied. If only, Ellie thought over and over, if only Pam cared more about winning! Or if she herself cared less!

Grandpa fortunately was too busy to become suspicious. For one thing, Mr. Sampson had arrived in time to see his gray, Foam, take second in the ladies' class and third in amateurs'. Ellie was satisfied with both performances, considering that she was riding against adults. Mr. Sampson, too, was pleased and paid her generously.

As the days rushed on, she pretended not to know that Challenger sensed a difference in her riding. Well, maybe not exactly in her riding, because so far she was doing her best. But more than most horses, he was sensitive to his rider's moods. She tried not to give him any hints of what she had decided to do, but she felt he guessed it from her tone, or her hands, or some small change of manner. Guilt made her so uncomfortable in his presence that she spent less time than usual with him. She noticed that he hurried through his meals, paying more attention to her than to his feed because he was afraid she would leave him. They were losing their bond of perfect closeness.

Not only at Barn B, but with all medal contestants, tension had increased. Nervousness took strange forms. Girls and boys who were ordinarily good-natured were growing irritable. Parents complained that children wouldn't eat, or couldn't sleep, or had turned downright unpleasant. Someone invented the phrase "mental class maniacs." Normally Ellie wouldn't have been nervous, because she had shown so often. But this time . . . Funny, she thought, she had never worried about winning, but here she was worrying about losing. Grandpa of course had to live up to his own opinion that nerves were foolishness. Still, he became darned fussy. Pam was the one least troubled, and she maddened Ellie by drifting off at the busiest moments to read movie magazines.

To ease the strain at least in their own group, Pam's parents arranged a supper party at the Date Tree. Along with the Sayres they invited the Bannisters and Mr. Sampson. As Mrs. Morton said smilingly, he would have a soothing effect on anyone. She planned they would eat out on the patio where the motel served meals. Here they could enjoy dinner music and watch the sun set over the desert.

To Ellie the evening was a real treat. She couldn't remember ever being at such an elegant party, in a beautiful setting, where people acted so gracious. As she relaxed at the candlelit table, she realized she had needed these few hours' recess.

"Isn't this the life, El?" Pam said lazily. Ellie could almost agree. Pam looked awfully pretty tonight, sort of glowing. She nudged Ellie as a woman passed, all dressed-up in shimmery green satin. "From Hollywood, I bet," she sighed. "Hear how she rustles! And umm, just smell her!" She sniffed rapturously.

Ellie too inhaled deeply, staring after the romantic vision.

"What are you two sniveling at?" Billy demanded.

Mr. Sampson was smiling at them across the table. "Don't be envious, young ladies," he advised. "Pam, you'll be the belle of the ball in a couple of years, and Ellie, those Irish eyes of yours are going to break hearts." His compliments were kind of embarrassing and old-fashioned, but evidently Pam loved them. She was posing, probably for his benefit, tilting her head in different positions and trying out ways of placing her hands. Mrs. Bannister too was trying to be most charming. She smiled so often that she seemed to have even more teeth than usual.

Ellie saw that Mr. Morton had finally broken the sound barrier of Mrs. Bannister's chatter to speak to Grandpa. Ellie caught the end of his sentence ". . . and this young couple, Pam's favorite cousins, will come from Los Angeles for the medal class Saturday."

"Riders?" Grandpa asked, eyes bright with interest.

"They're shopping for horses," Mr. Morton said. "They're eager to start showing, but they need instruction. Pam has improved so much that I suggested you might take them on. If Pam does well in the medal class, I'm sure they'll want to be among your clients."

Two new clients, Ellie thought, wow! After one glance at Grandpa's proud expression she resolved again not only would Pam do well, she would win.

Besides Mr. Morton's news, there were two other reasons why Ellie figured that Grandpa needed a winning pupil right now. First, the hunter hack loss hadn't done his reputation any good. People who had seen Challenger's performance blamed Grandpa for it. Of course they didn't know what had really happened, because he wouldn't explain about Bull Johnson's mean trick. That trick had forced Grandpa to scratch Challenger from his next class. Luckily it was only a trophy class. But even for money it would have been foolish to try showing him until he had forgotten the incident. It was plain that he hadn't. He acted suspicious in the warm-up area, snorty and shying in that particular corner of it.

The other special reason why Pam must win was that Grandpa had threatened to send Billy packing, after Billy told him a really whopping lie. Ellie knew that as always he meant what he said. It would hurt him to lose Billy as a customer, but having made his conditions he would stick by them.

One good thing, though, had come out of Billy's disgrace. His mother was so ashamed and so anxious to keep Billy with Grandpa that she became a great help to Ellie. Of her own accord she took over some of the housework and the trailer sparkled like new. She even washed and ironed clothes, mostly Grandpa's. This alarmed him.

With his passion for neatness, he appreciated the improvements, but he suspected Mrs. Bannister of trying to show what a fine wife she would make!

Thursday morning was the last schooling, what Pam called a dress rehearsal. Ellie wasn't surprised that Grandpa meant to skip schooling on Friday. He believed most horses and riders should relax the day before a big class. They should have a change of scene, like a leisurely ride away from the show grounds. Then they would come to their class fresh and rested instead of sour or tired. "Many's the class that's been lost," he would say, "by a horse who used up all his jump schooling."

Now he was going with the girls toward the ring. "Besides, if you and your horses aren't ready today," he said, "nothing we could do tomorrow would get you ready by day after tomorrow. So this morning I'm expecting your very best. Then this afternoon we'll run over some final questions. Tomorrow, both of you sleep late and enjoy a long slow ride, say through the palm groves, and don't think about showing."

"That'll be easy," Pam remarked.

"Not for me," said Ellie.

"Nonsense," Grandpa told her sharply. "Have you no control of your mind?" He added that Friday afternoon would be spent grooming both horses and checking over tack and clothes. "You're going in to your class spick and span to the last detail," he said. "The rules may read that in equitation classes only the rider's ability is considered. But a judge can't help being impressed by a rider who is neatly and suitably dressed, with clean tack and a well-groomed mount. That may be especially true of this judge, Mr. Prescott. He's an Easterner and no doubt he's used to more formality and precision than we are. He certainly won't look twice at anyone who's sloppy."

They had reached the ring, but Grandpa stopped at the gate. "Since I started this lecture, I'll finish it," he said. "Anyway the ring may be less crowded in a few minutes. Now what I said about sloppiness goes for your performance too. Don't go in there undecided or vague, gaping around or allowing your horse to. No, enter promptly when your number is called, at a businesslike walk. Then trot your circle as if you meant it. Pick up your canter—not a rocking chair lope but a good brisk hunting pace—and go at your fences with assurance. Go straight for the center of each one and remember, if you throw your heart over the fence, your horse will follow. That's courage."

Ellie thought about going in there fighting. She would this morning, she decided. As Grandpa started for the grandstand she said to Pam, "Come on, let's make him real proud. He deserves it."

"Just watch me," Pam said with a twinkle, and she rode into the ring, happily aware that the stands were nearly full.

They warmed up separately because talking while they warmed up was forbidden by Grandpa. For the next few minutes Ellie lost track of everybody and everything but Challenger, in her determination that he should do well. Right away he caught her mood, and she felt the old "togetherness" as strong as ever. For the first time since the hunter hack class he showed his true spirit. The thrill of being in perfect accord with him filled Ellie with something like a big swell of joy.

The fences had already been set in a figure eight by other riders who were practicing for the medal. Therefore Grandpa didn't come in, but signaled "Go ahead" from where he sat.

Ellie pulled to a stop and checked her girth. Then she began to circle at a walk near the gate, waiting for a chance to take the course without running into anyone. But Challenger was getting impatient. He was snatching for more rein, trying to break from his walk. When Ellie saw an opening coming, she let him trot. She completed a circle, broke into a gallop and headed for the brush with a warning yell, "Heads up!" He flew it clean, then angled across the ring to take the post-and-rails on the other wall, switching leads in the center. She steadied him at the far end, jumped the picket fence, crossed the center again for the brick wall. Almost before she knew it they were halfway through the second figure eight. He hadn't touched a thing and he had changed leads four times at just the right spot. Oh, he was going fine,

springy and bold but responding, not taking too much hold.

Ellie pulled up after eight fences. She couldn't help the big smile on her face. Even before she saw Grandpa's expression she knew by the other riders' that her performance had been first rate. Challenger knew it too. The way he strutted was positively cocky. He was a completely different horse from the sad and nervous one of the past few days. She wiped her damp face, blew back her bangs and licked the dryness from her retainer. Then she leaned to let the girth out a hole before she walked Challenger. Her eyes found Pam, who was waiting her turn at the jumps.

"Go on, go on," Ellie muttered unheard. "You have to grab your chance, no one's going to make it easy for you. Oh good, there you go, that's the girl! Hey, that's swell, you're doing fine . . . " She was holding her breath, watching Pam's slight figure on the flashy black mare. She had never seen Pam ride better! Her elbows were in, feet right, head up, her back hollowed just enough and hands perfect. Flight propped a little coming into the brick wall, but it wasn't her fault. A horse had crossed in front of her. Pam sent her right on, showing good horsemanship. They had a hind tick the second time over the picket, but it didn't matter, it wasn't anything. Then they had finished, and joined Ellie. "Did you watch?" Pam asked breathlessly. "Could you see? Did I look good?"

"You looked marvelous," Ellie told her, grinning.

Pam tossed her hair smugly. "I always do best before an audience."

It was true, Ellie realized. All the better for the medal class. "Come on," she said. "Grandpa's giving the 'that'll do' sign. Let's go hear about our crimes."

Even Grandpa couldn't complain of any crimes today, though he had observed that Ellie let Challenger trot instead of making him. Back at the barn he remarked gloomily that it was too bad things were going so well now. Still, there was time yet tomorrow for trouble, to get it over before Saturday. With a gratified air he studied Challenger and hummed his dismal favorite, "Farewell, Shamrock Shores."

That Thursday afternoon filled up unexpectedly. First someone ran over from another stable where a rider had just sprained an ankle. Ellie was asked to show his horse, which she did. It was a green one who couldn't possibly have placed, but she welcomed the experience and the pay. Then Grandpa, cautious as always, decided that a buckle on her girth needed fresh stitching. While he took it to the harness store in town, she replaced him coaching Billy. Altogether the day whizzed by. Night, though, passed slowly, at least for Ellie. She was disturbed by nightmares in which Challenger was arguing with her and tears were running down his face, and then her own tears woke her.

The nightmare feeling seemed to extend into Friday. Challenger was full of the high spirits he had shown ever since the successful dress rehearsal. His gaiety made Ellie feel all the more treacherous to him because she had given him a taste of triumph. Then all at once the weather turned scorching. Swimming was the only cure, said Pam, and she left for the motel right after their ride in the palm grove. Whether because of the heat or the prospect of the medal class, Ellie felt pale and limp. The tack-room mirror reflected her white face, emphasizing the freckles. Her hair stuck up damply and her cheek bones showed more than usual, as if she were getting thin.

"I'm a mess," she said to herself, coming out of the tack room that afternoon at feeding time. With a strange weariness she took up the pitchfork and went into Challenger's stall. Grandpa had followed her to the half door and stood watching, his cap drawn down over eyes that brooded in his tanned face.

"We won't blanket them tonight in this weather." He spoke absently, looking on while Challenger ate with enthusiasm in spite of the heat. "I'm glad to see him hungry," Grandpa said. "I was afraid he was commencing to lose weight. You know, he's a remarkable horse."

He didn't seem to expect an answer, so Ellie waited, leaning on the fork while she too watched her horse burying his nose in the pan of grain. The oats smelled good, and so did his warm coat, and the clean straw. Her glance traveled down to his white stockings. Tomorrow she would scrub them and shampoo his mane and tail. She would give him a bath all over, and braid him up real slick. At least he would look good. He would step into the ring the way she had seen him last Sunday, a great noble statue horse. And then. . . .

"Yes, a remarkable horse," Grandpa repeated. "Too sensitive for his own good. I can tell you this now, that ever since Bull Johnson's interference I've been afraid we'd have to scratch from the medal class. But since yesterday morning's schooling he's been a different horse. He needed that successful performance."

Of course Ellie knew how winning or losing affected Challenger. She also knew that her depression had depressed him, until yesterday. The subject was making her uneasy, but she couldn't resist asking what she had often wondered. "Do you think he thinks just exactly the way we do?"

Grandpa's blue eyes grew even more thoughtful and he took quite a long while to answer. "That's an interesting question—how nearly an animal's brain resembles a human's. I can't be sure, Ellen. All I know is that in Challenger's case he connects doing badly with being punished. He must have been cruelly abused in the past when he lost a class. Fear almost wrecked him for good, as you know. So now he needs to win, or at least to feel he's doing well." Grandpa's wrinkles crinkled in a smile. "If he should win that medal class tomorrow he'd be on top of the world."

"And you'd be on top of the world if Pam won." The words were out before Ellie realized they might sound suspicious. She was stunned when Grandpa answered calmly.

"I'd be pleased, naturally, if Pam won. It would be a good advertisement for my teaching. But it would be an even better advertisement to have Challenger win. Everyone knows what a nervous wreck he was a year ago. For us to have got him in shape to win a medal—well, now that would be something! And believe me, if he goes to pieces again, my rivals will make something of that too."

"They will?" Ellie said faintly. That hadn't occurred to her. In fact it was becoming clear that none of the right things had occurred to her, only wrong ones. "But what about Pam?" She asked. "If she doesn't win she might get discouraged and quit."

"That's a chance we have to take," Grandpa said stoutly. "If she has so little spunk—I might even say guts—that one failure discourages her, then she's not worth having as a pupil. At that, I'm not sure it would be best for her to win. Too much success too fast may go to her head. She reminds me of this lad I knew in Ireland . . ."

He went on talking, but Ellie didn't listen. Amazement and delight were chasing each other through her mind. It seemed impossible that all her worry about having to lose the class had suddenly vanished. Yet everything Grandpa had said was reasonable. How wrong she had been! And how close she had come to doing something dishonest. She saw now that God wasn't against her after all. He didn't need to make Challenger understand about losing because He had made her understand about winning.

With wild relief she threw her arms around Challenger's stomach. She pressed her face against him, murmuring crazy nonsense, listening to the rumble and stir of his insides as he ate. Then she raised her head to interrupt Grandpa gleefully. "Know something Grandpa? I'm stupid."

"Stupid?"

"Stupid," she repeated happily. She gazed out over the stall door and saw that the sky was just starting to turn pink. The evening no longer seemed stifling, but lovely with the glow of dusk. Peaceful sounds of munching came from up and down the aisle. Soon the carnival would light the night with color and music. The beautiful waltzy voice of the merry-go-round would tinkle, and the ferris wheel would sparkle among the stars. She kept staring out, foolishly patting Challenger's rump, raising tiny puffs of dust that floated on the golden air. Then she had a perfectly wonderful idea, one she had used before and always found thrilling.

"Oh Grandpa, let me sleep here tonight! Please, it'll be terrific! I'll bring out my blankets, and Challenger would love it. You know he's real careful of me. I mean it'll be so cool and nice," she babbled. "Besides, he and I have an awful lot to talk over. We want to plan exactly how to win the medal class."

Grandpa nodded, smiling. "You talk as if you didn't have at least a dozen rivals. Thirteen, by the program, to be exact. Seems to me you and Challenger are pretty sure of yourselves."

"Sure, we're sure." Ellie laughed, hugging Challenger again. "Remember, he has a proud name. We've got to see he lives up to it."

6. The Medal

"*F*IRST call for the medal class, hunt seat. First call. All medal class contestants to the ring. You have fifteen minutes."

"Hear the loudspeaker?" Ellie asked Challenger, as they stood together waiting in his stall.

From the next stall came Pam's voice, and now at last even she was nervous. "That announcer gives me the creeps. He sounds as if he's broadcasting the end of the world." She spoke to Flight, and Ellie noticed again how friendly Challenger was to Pam's voice. Right from the start he had liked her. Now Pam asked, "How's Challenger?"

"He's ready," Ellie answered. "You should see him. He knows. He wouldn't eat any breakfast, and he's been working himself up, you know, the way he does on a big day. It's as if he purposely gets himself to just the right point. He's looking toward the ring, with his ears pricked real sharp. His eyes are excited and he's snuffing in and out. He won't stand still, and I guess he doesn't need to any longer. It must be time to go."

Sure enough, there was Grandpa calling "Jocks up." At last the day, the hour, and now the fatal moment had arrived!

As both girls led out their horses Ellie had the impression that Pam looked shaky but awfully stylish in her britches and boots and black jacket. Flight too was stylish, with her coat glistening and the fine braids Ellie had given her this morning. As for Challenger, he looked gorgeous. He was bronze rather than chestnut since his bath. The white diamond could have been painted on his forehead and the stockings on his legs. Every braid was taut and matched to the last hair. His saddle and double bridle gleamed from Grandpa's "lick o' this and a lick o' that," and the stirrup irons and mouthpiece and curb chain were like new.

"If only it wasn't so hot," Pam was saying, mopping her face with a soggy tissue.

"Feeling a touch of nerves?" Grandpa asked her.

"Am I! I'm dying," she moaned.

His final words were for both girls. "It's good to be keyed up enough so you won't fall asleep on the job. Well, we've gone over everything, I'm sure—footing, pace, the angle of your fences, change of leads and all the rest. When you're called in afterwards to hack, don't let up. Remember classes have been decided on the hacking phase when scores were close. So now, good luck, both of you. Just do your best. That's all anyone can do."

Leaving the barn Pam said mournfully, "I have a hunch I'm going to fall off," and Ellie admitted, "It's my darn memory that bothers me. What if I forget the course? And oh death, where's my number?"

"Even you couldn't forget the course is a figure eight," Pam said with a feeble smile. "And you know perfectly well number nine is on your back."

For the tenth time Ellie reached up behind to make sure the round cardboard was securely hooked over the collar of her checked jacket. "Would it help if I made you mad?" she suggested.

"No, it's much too hot," Pam said crossly.

They reached the warm-up area as their class was receiving its second call. Ellie had to smile at the surprised way Challenger stared about while he circled with his rivals. They did look strange and solemn, the kids all dressed up and their mounts groomed to the last detail. No one spoke or smiled except Rolly Rawlings, whose cheeriness today was a little irritating. Friends and trainers too, forming a ring around the riders, were silent and plainly tense. In a way, Ellie thought, it was hardest on those who rode best. For them, though not for her, New York was just around the corner. She didn't care so much for herself that she couldn't go East. At least, not so terribly much. But for Challenger it would have been a swell trip. Just imagine if he made such a comeback that he could have shown, maybe won, in Madison Square Garden!

"Here, wake up," she told herself. Passing the ring gate she had seen that the best of the five-gaited class in there had been called out to work again on the rail. That meant they were almost finished.

She was trotting when the loudspeaker announced, "Last call for the medal class. All entries to the ring immediately. Last call." It did sound like the end of the world!

Ellie refused to let herself hurry. The gaited riders were still lined up for awards. Then her class would go in to jump one by one according to number. She was number nine so her turn wouldn't come for about fifteen minutes. She felt sorry for number one, a heavy girl wearing glasses. It was always tough to go first, and maybe discover there was a slippery spot or an extra sharp turn or some other new hazard in the ring.

The gaited class came out and the announcer said briskly, "Bring in the jumps, ring crew. Heads up at the

95

gate, please." With the others, Ellie moved aside while the flat-bedded truck hauled in the jumps. Then the ring crew fellows were setting them up—first the brush, then across to the post-and-rails, then around the far turn to the picket and across again to the brick wall. Watching from the gate, the riders made the usual complaints. "Aren't they huge!" "Look how they gleam! The fiends must have just painted them." "That brick wall's ten feet high. No wonder the photographer's taking his stand there. Photographers are like vultures. They always know where there's going to be a death." Somebody said, "I'm going to take the whole course with my eyes closed," and somebody else said, "I'm going to throw up." Rolly asked, "Did it ever strike you dopes that we don't have to do this?"

"I have to," Ellie answered him, "no matter how scared and miserable I am. Every time I feel like quitting, there's this thing inside me that makes me come back for more."

By chance she saw Grandpa watching her from the side lines. Mrs. Bannister was beside him, her mouth going like mad. He motioned Ellie to get busy, with words she could guess: "Are you working or playing?"

She left the group, collected Challenger and rocked off into a canter. He was feeling so good that she had to warn him to slow down. She could hardly bear to shorten his lovely bold stride, with his neck arched against the bit, and his muscles pumping in shiny waves, and the blowing he did when he felt high. Specks of foam flew from his blowing back on her, but it didn't matter. She would get Grandpa's help with the brush and rubrag before she went in. She gloated over the admiring expressions of people watching Challenger. The thud of his hoofs on the grass was like a song. Today the grass smelled dry, but good dry, like the stubble in a fresh cut hayfield. She wanted to take the edge off him but still conserve his high spirits. After three turns each way she pulled to a walk. Sweat had broken out on his neck, making the reins slippery. She could feel it too in the creases of her jodhpurs under her knees, and all down her back inside her shirt. Heat seemed to have dried her mouth, because she found it hard to swallow. It couldn't be that she was nervous . . . Ridiculous to get nervous . . . Oh well, as Pam would say, who wanted to swallow? Where was Pam, anyway? Oh, she was riding with Sid Andrews, chattering away now of all times. With her number four, she ought to be warming up seriously.

Even for Pam, Ellie wouldn't interrupt her own warming up. She kept walking, watching as much as possible every time she passed the ring gate. She saw number one refuse at the picket and nearly come off at the brick wall. Of course the horse's faults weren't supposed to count. Still, a bad performance made the rider look bad. Number two was Pete Dokes, the tall boy from Bakersfield. She knew he was an excellent rider. Today he appeared better than ever—horribly good, though maybe a tiny bit slow. Enthusiastic applause followed him when he rode out. She didn't see much of number three but she could tell by the short applause that he had been only fair.

Then there went Pam, and Ellie forgot herself. She crowded up to the gate and stood in her stirrups to see better. Pam was entering the ring just as Grandpa had advised, in a businesslike way, but she looked scared. Ellie held her breath while Flight jumped the brush, made a flying change of leads crossing the center, and sailed over the post-and-rails.

Challenger was studying the ring, and it was just as well to let him have a good look at it now. He stared in turn at each of the gaudy jumps as if measuring their height. His nostrils snuffed in and out, exploring the scents of dust, of sweating horses and humans. He inspected the white board sides of the ring which glared with reflected heat. His eyes took in the photographer, then Mr. Prescott the judge, who was striding about the center, alert to catch Pam's every motion over every fence.

"Good girl, keep it up, keep it up," Ellie murmured,

watching Flight clear the picket. "Now for that hateful brick wall . . . there they go . . . a front tick, but that's all right. Go on, the second round new . . . " She had backed a little away from the gate so that Challenger wouldn't attract Flight's attention. Classes had been lost on such details as a horse calling his stable mate at just the wrong moment. But she was close enough to see that Pam was smiling as she started her second round.

"It's going to be tough to beat her," Ellie told Challenger as Flight cleared the picket again. Turning back to the warm-up area, she was satisfied that Pam's performance was better than Pete Doke's.

Evidently Pam too was satisfied—too soon. The incredible happened. Ellie didn't see it, because she had left the gate, but she heard a chorus of groans from the audience. Shouts of "No!" No!" "The brick wall, the wall!" made her whirl in her saddle just as Pam reached the gate—finished, so she thought. She had skipped the last jump! It was impossible, and yet. . . .

"Off course, number four," the announcer said heartlessly. In stunned disbelief Ellie recalled Pam's own words, "Even you couldn't forget the course is a figure eight." The worst of it was, she had no time now to console Pam. She must give all her attention to Challenger.

The next few minutes were a jumble of time rushing,

rushing toward number nine's turn. Challenger was ready, Ellie knew. She herself was ready—or was she? She had to be, her turn was two away, one away, it was next. But oh death, number eight's horse hit the brick wall with a sickening crash. His rider lay sprawled without budging. People suddenly appeared in the ring and

for an endless interval stood around the fallen girl. Then the creepy voice said, "Heads up at the gate." A low growl announced the ambulance, and silent riders made way for it. Two white-dressed men jumped out, lifted the girl onto the stretcher and the stretcher into the ambulance. Somebody, probably a relative, hurried to get in too. Then the long gray motor glided out, and a minute later its wail was heard headed for the hospital.

"So what's a little spill?" Ellie said with a soothing hand on Challenger's neck. Not that he was upset by the commotion. On the contrary, he had stood watching and plainly decided that since he trusted his rider, such an accident couldn't happen to him. It must have been for herself that Ellie was saying, "The horse wasn't hurt. See? They're leading him out. Let's get up to the gate again. That's it. Look, they've fixed the brick wall. It's only silly old pretend bricks. They couldn't hurt anybody. On your toes now. Ready?" She licked her dry lips and tried to breathe normally so that her heart would slow its thumping.

"Number nine," the announcer called. "Number nine, Challenger. Owned and shown by Ellen Sayre."

In the next second, a single voice came clear, ". . . beautiful, but will he perform?"

Would he! she thought. Whoever doubted it had an awful nerve. With a determined jerk she settled her cap more firmly, tightened her reins and legs. The gates swung open. She urged Challenger in.

A big flat-footed walk now, as both of them took a last purposeful look at the course. All right, collect him, and into a brisk trot. The circle was completed, so off into the gallop. No rocking chair lope, but a strong hunting pace, and straight for the middle of the brush. Four strides, three, two, and take off. Give him rein, he's jumping big. Fine, and now across to the other side. Change leads in the center. That was great. Hey, take back, we're not racing. Here comes the post-and-rails. Wow, did we ever clear it! Easy for this far turn, and straight for the picket. No, no, the middle of it, the middle! Here, quick, take back to cross the center again. That was perfect. Now watch out, here comes the brick wall. Oh, it's enormous! More rein, he has to jump big. Feel him gather? Get set—now—now! Good grief, he must have jumped five feet! Hear the people? Oh Challenger, you're a wonder, you're the only horse in the world!

Amid breathless silence in the stands Ellie started the second round. The wind of motion stung her eyes and the taste of excitement filled her mouth. But she felt marvelous, solid and strong as Challenger himself under her. Only, did she look all right? It was funny how you could think so much in just seconds, like a drowning man reviewing his whole life. Is my back right—my feet—hands? Mustn't look at them . . .

The brush whisked by underneath, the little toy post-and-rails was passed, the picket had been left behind. In a weird drowning-man flash Ellie glimpsed the packed stands, hands still but raised ready to clap. Here and there a bright dress stood out, or an arm fanning with a program. Glare from the side boards was dazzling, and it seemed that in the second of switching leads for the last time, here in the center there was a well of heat. Foam flicked from Challenger's arched neck, drops fell from under Ellie's cap, dust filmed her teeth and blurred her eyes. Sickness rose in her and she thought distinctly, I'm getting dizzy. Her voice said hoarsely, "Don't you dare."

As she spoke Challenger faltered. The wall loomed, big as a house, and his doubt became her doubt. With that instant's loss of speed they would never make it. She was afraid to try. Temptation to stop here swept her. Then the thought flashed: Throw your heart over and he'll follow. She sent Challenger on, hard. The wall rushed at them and he gathered himself, but too late, surely too late. Her body felt the effort of his, and she bent almost double to give him rein. The huge leap carried him high where he seemed to hang while the photographer's bulb flashed. She listened for the crack of wood but heard only her own gasp. Next second he had landed in a perfect arc. He was breezing on, eager for more, for bigger, wider, tougher fences, anything she asked!

Ellie straightened to thunderous applause. It roared around her and rose wave on wave, and there were shouts of "Good girl!" "Well done," and better yet, "What a horse!" That was the point—what a horse! While she left the ring solemnly, all at once a big lump filled her throat and something like tears made her blink. Out of pure pride for Challenger she could have cried.

Only there was no time to cry, or to laugh either. In the warm-up area Ellie slid off and found herself surrounded by a flattering crowd. The Bannisters were there, Billy jumping up and down; and Pam, repeating "Oh Ellie, oh Ellie"; and Pam's cousins, the young couple named Nelson who wanted to start showing. But in all the confusion Ellie really saw only Grandpa, and listened only to him saying, "Yes, you did a pretty fair job." His face said a lot more, but he wouldn't take time now to talk. Ellie understood, especially when he added mildly, "That last fence was a bit of a problem, wasn't it?"

While the remaining four riders were jumping, she and Grandpa brushed, dusted and sponged both herself and Challenger. They mustn't go in damp and messy for the hacking phase, or for the questions Mr. Prescott might ask after he lined up the class. Ellie was dying to dash to the ringside and see how the last riders were doing, but she was too busy. Also she didn't want to leave Challenger. She wished she could act more like him, pleased and cocky instead of all trembly and limp.

Now a new worry attacked her. It was the silence while the final rider jumped. Not only the silence, but then the clapping which followed his exit. He must have been about perfect. She was tempted to ask Grandpa whether she or this rider had received more applause, but somehow the question seemed unsporting.

Three minutes later the contestants were riding it off, all but the injured girl and Pam, whose mistake had disqualified her. At first Challenger kept looking for jumps. Ellie quieted him by voice and by purposely relaxing herself, so that after a turn of the ring she was able to concentrate on her horsemanship. Forcing herself to look straight ahead, she couldn't keep track of Mr. Prescott. When he lined up the class she had no idea with what kind of expression he had watched her. Maybe he had simply overlooked her. Maybe he wouldn't place her because she had lost her number. If it was still on her, wouldn't she feel it? Her fingers tingled to reach back and make sure but she ignored the urge. Also she ignored Sue Andrews next to her.

"Don't look now, Ellie," Sue was saying. "I'll report on him." "Him" was Mr. Prescott, of course. "Don't you move. It doesn't matter what I do after all I already did wrong."

Without moving her lips, Ellie made a questioning sound.

"Oh, everything," Sue groaned. "You name it, I did it. As for poor Pam, I thought she'd be planning to cut her throat for missing that fence. But all she's worried about is having looked like a fool. She can't wait to prove at Santa Barbara that she really knows better."

"Mmm," Ellie mumbled, pleased with Pam's spirit. She rolled her eyes toward the judge and mumbled again. "What's he mmming?"

"He's thinking," Sue reported. "He isn't asking any questions. He's checking his score card and looking us all over, moving this way. Don't let Challenger budge an inch, he's perfect."

Ellie felt that the strain of waiting was more than she could bear. In a way she was glad she couldn't see the last rider, the good one. The sight of him would be depressing. She stared ahead at the reserved box where the Western judge and other officials were sitting. They were talking and pointing to different riders in the line-up. At the front of the box were set gleaming trophies and the rack of many-colored ribbons. Oh, those gor-

geous blues! By squinting she could make out one small
square case which must contain the medal. She knew
what it looked like—a beautiful silver circle, about four
inches across, engraved with the words AMERICAN
HORSE SHOWS ASSOCIATION. Under the words was a
winged horse rearing up among the clouds. She could
just feel that medal in her hand, rich and heavy and—

"Look out, he's coming," Sue warned.

Sneaking a sideways glance, Ellie saw Mr. Prescott
approach and stand in front of Sue. He studied his score-
card, frowned, studied Sue, pursed his lips, then came on
to stop before Challenger. Looking straight over his
head, Ellie could still see that he was tall and well-
dressed, medium aged, with gray hair and a face that
meant no nonsense. There was no nonsense about Challenger either. He was doing his statue pose, motionless
in the sunshine as a horse carved from bronze. Motionless he remained while Mr. Prescott looked over the last
entry, marked his card, handed it to the announcer and
joined the other officials. He was actually heartless
enough to light a cigarette!

The manager stepped out from the box. He was going
to present the medal himself. Someone handed him the
mike. The photographer appeared, and his presence was
like a signal for silence. There wasn't a sound from the
stands, from the ring, from the watchers at the gate.

Even the horses were quiet, only one or two rolling their bits in the stillness.

"Ladies and gentlemen," the manager began, "you are about to learn the results of the American Horse Shows Association hunt seat medal class, judged by Mr. Howard Prescott of Westbury, Long Island. This is an extremely important event, important particularly to the winner, who will be eligible to compete this fall in the finals at Madison Square Garden."

He paused impressively, and Ellie heard herself whisper, "Never mind, honey. As far as I'm concerned you've won. You won it right there at the brick wall where it took so much nerve. So don't be sad if—Oh, but they will, they've got to! Only people make mistakes, so don't be disappointed if—"

"I take great pleasure," the manager said.

I take great pleasure, Ellie's mind echoed.

"In presenting this medal . . ."

In presenting this medal . . .

". . . to one whom we all . . ."

. . . *whom we all*—Hey, wait, what was wrong? The manager was still talking but Ellie couldn't catch his words because Challenger was distracting her. The audience too was acting funny, suddenly all looking at her and talking at once. She felt her face turn red as embarrassment flooded her.

"No, Challenger," she begged, trying to stop him. Some of the people were laughing now, everyone clapping and clapping, all those heads turned her way, all those faces smiling.

Really they were smiling at Challenger. He had stepped forward even before Ellie's name was called. Now she was receiving the medal. Sunlight glinted on it, but no more brightly than on his fiery coat. His neck was arched in silky curves, his ears were pricked to the applause, his steps were proud. Plainly he knew he was the champion. Just like the winged horse among the clouds, Challenger was on top of the world!

7. A Bargain

TWO weeks later, stretched on the beach at Santa Barbara, Ellie felt as if she were in another world. It wasn't at all like the country they had left. The showgrounds here were within sound of the surf. They were between blue, blue sea and tall mountains. The town was quaint, its buildings were mostly adobe in the old sections. The famous Mission looked down from the hill where Indians had built it over a hundred and seventy-five years ago. Gardens were fragrant with brilliant blue jacaranda trees, pink eucalyptus and sunny cup o' gold. At night you walked out on the quay, barefoot on the splintery still-warm planks. Or you raced along the beach, close to the water where the hard sand squeaked underfoot. You watched the harbor lights, and all the boats there, fishing boats and yachts and sometimes sailing ships. You imagined distant lands and ports and foreign languages.

A Bargain

You remembered stories about pirates. And somehow all these sights and the strange smells and different sounds made you wonder about the whole world. . . .

Ellie pushed herself up onto one elbow to talk to Pam, lying within arm's reach. But Pam was asleep, looking just like a picture in a magazine. She had spread a towel under her shining hair and oiled herself with suntan lotion. Her swim suit was a one-piece flowered print which matched the cute beach bag that held toilet articles, cap and movie magazines.

Ellie lay back again, lulled almost to sleep herself by the pounding waves and salty air and the faint cries of seagulls and of children playing with sand castles and seaweed. Her mind drifted over the past weeks and all that had happened since she won the medal. Or since Challenger won it, she thought with a smile, remembering how he had stepped up to claim it and how embarrassed she had been at the time. Everyone had teased her afterward, even while they congratulated her for having the smartest horse on the grounds. Challenger obviously agreed with them. Since he had won, his spirits had risen steadily. He had discovered the meaning of fun. The first time he tried a small playful buck Ellie was so astonished that she nearly fell off. Naturally she understood that his contentment was due to his victory. She intended that he should win several more classes here. Not the medal of course, that must go to Pam whom she had been coaching since they persuaded Grandpa that Pam's lessons would be more fun that way.

"Fun?" he had said, at first suspicious of such a flighty notion. As soon as he saw they were serious, he hadn't interfered. He considered the experiment good experience for both girls. Ellie was specially pleased when he agreed, because she wanted practice coaching, preparing for the time when maybe he would accept her as his assistant. That would be the first stage of becoming a trainer herself—her favorite dream. Already she had done well at teaching Billy, and had made the satisfying discovery that being a trainer, rather than merely a rider, was a real thrill. It gave you importance and responsibility, and required brains instead of mostly muscles.

"Hey, El, what time is it?" Pam's drowsy voice interrupted her thoughts.

"Time to go home, I bet," she answered, sitting up. Home meant the trailer, three blocks inland. It was home to both, for Pam had moved in. By great good luck, as she said, her brother in Los Angeles had come down with the mumps. Her parents had rushed home, leaving her with the Sayres.

"Don't you love Santa Barbara?" she sighed, walking

along. She didn't really expect an answer. "I hear this is the most glamorous show on the circuit."

"Yes, partly because it's a night show," Ellie replied, "with lights and music and everything. People in the boxes will be all dressed up, the ladies in evening gowns and furs and jewels and the men in tuxedos. But it's a shame it's too swank to have a carnival."

"Maybe there'll be some movie actors?" Pam asked.

"Oh, yes. Last year we had Rock Hunter and Dawn O' Day."

"Umm, dreamy," Pam murmured.

"I'd rather meet Lassie or Trigger," Ellie said.

Pam sniffed. "Them! Kid stuff."

"You know," Ellie said as they reached the grounds, "these two weeks have been swell, with not much to do and no one much here, except that nasty Bull Johnson."

"Bull Johnson's the trainer who has those two crazy skinny jumpers, isn't he?" Pam asked. "I hadn't noticed that he was nasty."

Ellie would have liked to explain about him. She and Pam told each other everything nowadays, but she didn't dare disobey Grandpa.

The trailer came in sight. "I have a suspicion Grandpa's secretly glad the Bannisters'll get here tonight," Pam said, "He misses Mrs. B's housework, in spite of all her teeth and talk. He told me—" she giggled— "that since I moved in, the trailer looks as if a tornado had hit it."

"One good thing about Mrs. Bannister," Ellie said, "is that Challenger likes her."

Pam smiled. "How can you tell? And how come you always claim to know what he feels?"

On the warm sidewalk Ellie stopped to think out loud. "You don't understand. I guess no one exactly understands about Challenger and me . . . except maybe Grandpa, and even he said once that it's an interesting question how much horses think like humans. Well, about Challenger it's no question to me. See, I *know*." She paused, pushing at her bangs while she tried to express the difficult thought. "The thing is, sometimes I practically *am* Challenger. When he's afraid, I'm sick at my stomach, and when he's sad I get an ache in my chest. I'm friends with the same people and hate the same people he does. When he's worrying, I can't eat at the same time he won't touch his feed pan. And when he's happy, the way he was after he won the medal—Pam, if it wouldn't sound crazy, I'd say that day he talked to me. I knew, I just knew, that's all, how people and other horses, everything, looked to him. He kind of danced on the grass as if it was greener than ever before, and he sniffed at those silly palm trees as if they smelled marvelous, and he pricked his ears at ordinary type birds who sang like—like larks or something." Walking on again Ellie smiled, remembering that afternoon and how Challenger had actually bucked with joy.

The trailer stood where a shady little park met the show grounds on their seaward side. Here its electric cord was plugged into the last electric outlet on the shed row. Grandpa had chosen this spot so as to get more sleep and quiet, away from the ring. Too, it was sheltered from both fog and heat by Tamale Hill, which skirted the grounds on one side and ended just beyond the trailer.

That evening Grandpa told the girls that tomorrow they must get along without him. He was expecting Pam's cousins, the Nelsons, with whom he planned to look over some horses. As soon as the young couple were suitably mounted they hoped to start showing in amateur classes. Though Ellie was used to having less help from him these days, she was tempted to ask his advice about a problem that had been bothering her. It would be more satisfying though to solve it herself, and she decided to have a last good try tomorrow.

Next morning after early chores she had Pam saddle Flight and she followed them afoot to the ring. She could criticize best from the grandstand as Grandpa did. It was fascinating how much you learned about horses by studying someone else on them.

They had the ring to themselves, so Ellie raised her voice to coach Pam. "I have a hunch what the trouble is. If you'll take two or three fences after warming up, I'll watch real close and make sure. There's got to be a reason why Flight drags her hind legs over the jumps with you. She never used to."

"It's lucky faults don't count in equitation," Pam answered.

"I know, but they don't help," Ellie said. "Besides, we can't let her get set in a bad habit. She's got so that often as not she rolls off a pole behind. It's always behind."

From the far end of the ring Pam called, "It's sure to be my fault."

"Most likely it is," Ellie called back, "but it's my fault not seeing what you're doing wrong."

One thing Pam was doing right these days was paying strict attention to her horsemanship. Probably the reason was that here she had had no audience. This morning there were only a couple of men looking on idly from a distance. The real test of her attention would come before a full grandstand, when she would be tempted to watch the spectators for admiring looks. She had promised not to give in to that temptation. In a really convincing way she had said, "I'm going to show people I'm not as stupid as I acted when I went off course last time." Her big brown eyes had been wistful as she sighed. "I'd give anything to hear, just once, that glorious applause all for me!" At that very moment she had resolved "New York or bust."

Ellie had two post-and-rails ready by the time Pam had warmed up. Now like Grandpa she ordered "Go ahead." Flight cleared the first fence neatly in front, but again dropped her hind legs in mid-air just enough to roll off the top rail.

"Keep going," Ellie called. She was almost sure she had found Pam's fault. When the same thing happened at the second fence, she motioned Pam to the center.

"I think I've got it," she said. "You're sitting back too soon. See, you get forward all right for the take-off, but a horse still needs lots of rein after he's in the air. You straighten too soon, and when you drop your weight back, she drops those hind legs. Get it?"

It was terribly interesting, and Ellie thought it over later while she saddled Foam. "We'll go to the beach," she told him. "The salt water's good for your legs. And you," she said to King, "stick your fat face into this halter so I can lead you."

Riding over the deep sand toward the sea was the funniest sensation. Like riding a camel in the Sahara, Ellie imagined. Then where the sand hardened it was springy. The horses' hoofs made a slapping noise on it. She coaxed them out where after each wave the water slid forward in foamy scallops. First they sidled in where it curled around their feet. Then they went in up to their knees, then to their bellies. You could make yourself dizzy by staring straight down at the swirling green water. And you could give yourself a marvelous reckless feeling by galloping fast, with a great pounding and splashing, where the beach stretched ahead, miles and miles of gorgeous white sand. On one side the whole

A Bargain

Pacific ocean sparkled at you and on the other the mountains reached for the sky. You could let yourself go in the craziest way, like singing or yelling, for there was no one to hear but a few fishermen and gulls.

Late next afternoon in the trailer the girls were discussing Mrs. Bannister. Mrs. Bannister evidently had determined to prove that Grandpa couldn't get along without her. She was doing a fine job of it too. The medal was a week and a half off. Already in today's schooling Pam's posture had improved. Now she was studying the rule book. Or she was supposed to be studying in her upper bunk. At the moment she had hung her head over the edge in order to see Ellie below. Her face looked a little purplish, upside down between curtains of hair.

On the lower bunk Ellie was mending a torn pocket while they discussed the fascinating subject of Mrs. Bannister. She stood up, peered from the windows, then into Grandpa's room. Sitting down again, she lowered her voice. "Do you think she wants to marry him?"

"At their age?" Both considered the amazing idea. And yet . . .

"She's a swell housekeeper," Ellie pointed out. "Grandpa would never have to ask her if she was working or playing! And she'd be company for him, and it would be good for Billy."

Pam's face was solemn. Her hair swung from side to side as she shook her head, puzzled by the problem. Maybe they could give Mrs. Bannister a hint not to talk so much. But that would be difficult without insulting her, which they didn't want to do because really she was a nice person. For instance, she had decided to copy Mrs. Morton and add variety to the week with a supper party. All today she had worked over sandwiches and salads and fruit punch. She had managed to bake a sponge cake in the trailer oven and had even provided a thermos to be filled with black tea for Grandpa. She planned that tonight they would take a picnic up on Tamale Hill. There would be a new moon. "Very romantic," she had said with a smile meant no doubt to be girlish. Pam and Ellie had been dazzled less by the smile than by the array of teeth it revealed. Feeling mean, they had smothered their giggles. There had been much argument about whether to hold the picnic on the hill or at the beach. But they had all been to the beach repeatedly, especially Ellie with the horses. And now Pam spent as much time there riding as she used to spend just sun bathing.

It pleased Ellie that Grandpa had noticed the improvement in Pam's attitude, her new determination. But he never forgot the medal class coming closer every day, or his responsibility for Pam. Only yesterday he had spoken to Ellie, privately and seriously, about Pam's progress.

A Bargain

Ellie admitted there was a problem in horsemanship that
troubled them. Suddenly doubting her own ability she
had said, "Maybe I better explain it to you. You could
correct it quickly."

"Maybe I could," he answered. From under his cap he
looked down at her, evidently deep in thought while he
hummed the "Rose of Tralee." At last he went on.
"That would be the easy way. But wouldn't it be wiser
for you to work this out yourself? I won't be around so
many more years to advise you, so you'd better begin
learning to rely on your own judgment. Provided of
course that you're still helping Pamela. Otherwise I'd
take over at once." He laid a hand on Ellie's shoulder,
and she knew by the gentleness of his touch and tone
that he was speaking straight from his heart. "I've been
proud of you, Ellen, of the way you've come along
under my coaching. I'd like to go on being proud, feeling that you are growing mentally as well as physically.
It's been my hope that some day you would join me in
the business." Exactly her hope too!

He hesitated, then continued as if he was figuring his
way along. "You've done so well with both Pamela and
Billy, and of course with Challenger, that I was even
considering, this coming winter . . . But first you'd
have to show me how you would deal with this fault of
Pamela's, whatever it is. If you can correct it and keep

her improving—well, I see no reason why you shouldn't go on coaching her right through the medal. You're young to be teaching, but you have a knack of reaching Pamela better than I do. Perhaps it's youth . . . or being two girls together. But a medal class is a tough test. I'm not sure you can handle it."

"Oh, I'll handle it all right," Ellie had said quickly, wanting to end their talk before Grandpa changed his mind. But something he had said bothered her, and she had to tell him. "Don't say you won't be around many more years. You're—uh, spry as anything."

"Flattery will get you nowhere, miss," he had retorted, gruff but pleased. "Let's see how you'll pass this test."

Now from the upper bunk of the trailer Pam started down to get ready for the picnic supper. Ellie went to open the door, expecting Mrs. Bannister. Grandpa was taking a last look around, and locking the tack room. He headed for the trailer just as the others drove up—Bannisters, Nelsons, and Mr. Sampson in a car as prim and old-fashioned as he and Foam were.

Pam giggled at his greeting, delivered with a bow and a sweep of his hat. "Good evening, all—young ladies, friend Patrick, Mrs. Bannister and escort . . ."

"I'm escort?" Billy asked.

A Bargain

". . . and ah, our young lovers!" For as usual the Nelsons were hand in hand.

Billy was pleased with his title. "That's my name," he announced. "Escort. Everybody remember."

A few minutes later Mrs. Bannister chirped, "Ready now?" She was surveying her group like a Den Mother shepherding Cub Scouts. "All right, single file up the trail, and careful of poison oak. The youngest first . . ."

"That's me!" shouted Escort.

". . . and we older folks will bring up the rear," his mother concluded with a gay glance at Grandpa.

They marched off, singing "Row, Row, Row Your Boat" by order of their Den Mother. Judging from the sounds behind her, Ellie was afraid Pam would get hysterical and hurt Mrs. Bannister's feelings.

The climb and the beauty of the balmy evening brought a hush over the whole group as they toiled uphill. By the time they reached a suitable flat spot near the top, everybody was glad to sink down on the still-warm, dry grass. Food tasted awfully good, especially with a sensational view to enjoy while they ate.

Lights were springing on in the harbor as if to reflect the stars beginning to twinkle above. The little boats spoke back and forth in their own language of bells and whistles. The ocean was quiet in the still dusk; only the breakers fell with a boom far out. After a minute, their edges hissed up over the sand, then they were sucked back again. The smell of sea mingled with the tangy smell of sage which grew all around. Directly below, the ring and stables lay in darkness, but now and then a horse neighed or pawed or rattled a feed pan.

Ellie was hoping, after supper, that Mrs. Bannister found the setting romantic enough, for now a slim white slice of moon had slipped up over the mountains to silver the earth's highlight and blacken its shadows. The Nelsons of course always brought their own atmosphere of romance. Mr. Sampson had dozed off, neatly propped against a tree stump. Pam's eyes were following the headlights of the cars on the distant highway. They must have made her think of traveling, for she said something to Mrs. Bannister about how determined she was to see New York. Mrs. Bannister for once wasn't talking. She and Billy had been enjoying Grandpa's tales of when he was a lad walking hots at the Leopardstown track.

Lying on her back, Ellie listened to the throb of crickets' voices and stared at the moon and thought about Challenger. After a time she heard a horse neigh below in the stable and she recognized his voice. She went to stand listening a few feet from the others. After a moment Grandpa joined her.

"Whose voice was that?" he asked. She guessed he was testing her.

"Challenger's," she answered.

"Is he in trouble?"

"Oh no. I can tell from his tone he's all right." She made out that Grandpa was nodding, evidently satisfied. Thinking aloud she went on. "It's terribly interesting how well I understand him. . . . So for you it must be ten times more interesting having lots of people's horses to understand and train. . . ." Envying him reminded her of her own hopes of someday being a trainer. And that reminded her that he had *started to say* something about hoping, this coming winter . . . But first, he'd said, she would have to prove she could handle Pam in the medal class.

She had been stupid. He had been getting confidential, and she had let him stop. Surely what he had been going to say about next winter couldn't be the exciting thing she wished . . . Still, with his business growing he needed help, at least part time, giving lessons and so forth back home when the show circuit ended. And he was satisfied with her coaching of Billy and Pam. He wouldn't be satisfied though unless Pam really performed in the medal here. That was to be the tough test.

Suddenly she faced Grandpa with a little gasp of excitement. "I have an idea," she said. "It's perfectly terrific. It's a bargain, see."

"Yes?" His voice was cautious.

"I thought—well, here's the first part. If Pam does well in the medal, it will prove I'm a good trainer, won't it?"

"I'd say yes, it will." He was even more cautious, as if he suspected a trap.

"So here's the bargain." Ellie took a big breath and said quickly, "If she does well in the medal you'll take me next winter as your assistant."

"Here, not so fast," Grandpa warned, and she felt a stab of dismay. "What about your school work?"

"Oh, I'll have plenty of time, plenty!" she assured him.

"Well, but we'd have to get permission at home."

We! He had said *we*. She knew she was gaining. "That'll be easy," she said. "Oh Grandpa, come on, do it. Please do it."

For ages Grandpa was silent, looking down at her. At last he moved and reached out a hand. "It's a bargain," he said, and by starlight they solemnly shook hands.

8. Disaster

---

*T*HE morning after the picnic was another of those sparkling clear ones that make you feel nothing bad could possibly happen today. In her lower bunk Ellie allowed herself five minutes' laziness after she woke. No one was up, but she could hear Challenger moving about in his stall. He would be pushing at the straw with his nose, a hint that it was breakfast time. As soon as he caught sight or sound of her he would nicker, and that would signal all his friends in Grandpa's stable to start hollering for food and water. Then everyone might as well get up. In fact, it was too nice a day to waste any of it, Ellie decided. With a last mighty stretch and yawn she threw back her covers and reached into Pam's bunk to tickle her awake. "New York or bust," she reminded her.

"Oh, bust," Pam groaned.

For Pam's lesson today they planned to use only Challenger. Ellie wanted to do the riding, to demonstrate again good and bad posture over fences. But as they reached the ring her famous memory began to bother her. She couldn't remember whether she had properly closed Foam's door, on which the latch was loose. "I'll have to go check," she said and slid off Challenger. "Here, you walk him a few minutes. I'll be right back."

"You mean ride him, me?" Pam exclaimed. She looked so pleased that Ellie couldn't say no, she had meant lead him. Ordinarily she wouldn't want anyone else to ride him, and neither would he. But he had always trusted Pam, and he did now as she reached eagerly for the stirrup to mount. He only turned his head, the foretop flicking over the white diamond as he glanced back at her as if to say, go ahead.

It was lucky that Ellie returned to Foam's stall. His door was closed all right, but he had been playing with the latch again, and now it must be mended. Scolding him, she fetched screws from the tack room and went to work. She had the repairs nearly completed when Pam's voice startled her. It sounded panicky.

"Ellie! Oh, Ellie, come quick." Pam arrived running, stumbling in her haste. Her face was white, her words frightened. "Oh, something awful's happened! I didn't mean to, I didn't know, but he said he'd help and I let him and—"

Ellie slammed the door of Foam's stall and whirled to grab Pam's arm. "What happened?" she cried. "Who said he'd help? Where's Challenger?"

Pam broke out crying and couldn't answer. She looked so upset that Ellie decided she had had an accident. "You fell off! Oh Pam, you're hurt!"

"No, no, it's not me—"

"Then it's Challenger." Ellie shook Pam's arm. "Where is he?"

"I'll show you," Pam said. She turned to lead the way then hesitated.

"Get going," Ellie ordered, "and tell me while we go."

"The thing is," Pam began, moving unwillingly, "I'm afraid you'll be—you'll have a—a shock."

Ellie felt herself turn pale and sort of sick. With stiff lips she stammered, "What's wrong with him?"

Pam was hurrying now. She half-turned her face away. "He's down, and he can't—well, he can't get up. One leg—I think one leg—"

"Oh no!" The words burst from Ellie like a cry of pain. For a second she stopped, staring at Pam from eyes that felt stretched by fright. Then she managed to ask, "Where?"

"Back of Barn G," Pam said, and she started after Ellie who had broken into a frantic run.

Behind her, Ellie could hear Pam trying to explain. "Remember those two men who watched me jump day before yesterday, when Flight kept rolling off the pole? The big one was Bull Johnson. I met him just now while I was on Challenger. He said he could show me an easy way to do better. He wanted to help."

"You stupid dope," Ellie muttered, careless that she was unfair since Pam knew nothing about Bull Johnson.

"So," Pam panted on, "he took us into his aisle behind Barn G. He had me get off, and he put up a jump."

"How high?" Ellie snapped over her shoulder.

"Oh, high. Too high," Pam said miserably. "Then he snapped a long rope to Challenger's headstall and chased him over the jump. At least he meant to, but somehow he scared Challenger and then everything happened. Challenger hit the jump, and it must have been solid because it broke instead of falling. You never heard such a crash. He fell, with kind of an awful grunt and—"

"You shouldn't have left him," Ellie said, again unfair because how else would she have known what had happened? She didn't want to hear any more. Neither did she want to see what was waiting behind Barn G. But they were almost there. They were turning the corner. She wanted desperately to close her eyes, not to look down that aisle. But she looked and—she saw him.

He was alone by the wrecked jump in the deserted aisle. He was up, but standing in a funny way. Coming from behind, Ellie hardly recognized her horse. His head was low, his coat stained with sweat and dust. He made no sign of welcome at her step. Closer, she saw the ground was churned by his struggles to get up. Pieces of the jump were flung all over. She forced herself to walk around in front, dreading to look at his forelegs because of the way he was standing.

Then she was facing him, and all at once everything started to waver in the sunlight. She heard a far off cry in her own voice, then she heard Pam sob, "I wish I was dead."

"I wish you were!" she answered wildly while dizziness blurred the sight of beautiful white stockings turned bright red.

Ellie wondered afterward why she as well as Pam hadn't cried at sight of Challenger's legs red with blood. She supposed she was too shocked. Also, there wasn't time.

Half on purpose, half from faintness, she collapsed on her knees in front of him. For the first time he noticed her, and lowered his head still more to touch her hands. Very gently she felt his legs, in spite of the blood. Her finger tips explored his knees, then down his cannon bones, his fetlocks, his feet. She pressed cautiously, watching his face. She couldn't feel any break, but he kept flinching. Naturally, even with no bones broken, those poor legs would hurt like anything. Each was gashed just below the knee where he must have hit the fence. Pain from the gashes made him shift from foot to foot as if his weight was unbearable.

Disaster

Ellie scrambled to her feet, unsnapped the trailing rope and picked up Challenger's dangling reins. That fiendish Bull Johnson hadn't even bothered to halter and unsaddle him for jumping! She examined the rest of him which was all dusty and sweaty but seemed otherwise all right. Yet he wasn't like himself at all, or not like the proud self he had lately become. She thought with despair that right now he could only be called pitiful.

"We can't stay here," she said, looking around anxiously. She wasn't sure he ought to move, for blood was still oozing from his gashes. But these should be cleaned and disinfected immediately. She should get the vet—but was there one on the grounds, and who was he, and was he good? Oh, if only Grandpa were here, instead of horse hunting with Pam's cousins! There was no one in sight, except Pam still tearful. Ellie turned her back on her and coaxed Challenger. "Come on, honey. Don't be afraid, it's all over. Please—you can walk, can't you? Try."

The trip back took forever. Ellie felt that every step was hurting her. When at last Challenger saw his stall he tried to hurry, and the effort was pathetic. Foam called him and he answered in a sad imitation of his usual voice.

Inside the stall Ellie tied him and ran for a bucket of water and clean cloths. Silently Pam removed his saddle and bridle. She remained silent while Ellie washed his legs and applied Grandpa's disinfectant. Scarcely glancing at Pam, Ellie said, "Better rub him down." She left Pam working with scraper and rubrag, and ran off to the horse show office. Although is wasn't officially open, she hoped someone would be around who could advise her about a vet. It couldn't be helped that vets were expensive. Without Grandpa she really had no idea what to do for Challenger, and she wasn't taking any chances that he would get worse. Certainly he needed an antitetanus shot or he might have blood poisoning; then he might—well, horses could die from that.

"Stop thinking and hurry!" she gasped, running as hard as she could.

Ten minutes later she was running again, back to the barn. All she had done was make several useless phone calls and receive suggestions from strangers. She found Challenger at least dry and clean. The blood had stopped oozing but his knees were beginning to swell. She decided cold water might keep down the swelling. As she started to lead him to the wash rack at the end of the aisle, Pam asked what to do next. "You've done enough," Ellie snapped. "You crippled my horse. I suppose you'd like to kill him!"

Disaster

"Oh, for heaven's sake!" said Pam with an indignant flounce.

A half-hour's hosing did seem to reduce the swelling. When Ellie led Challenger slowly back to his stall, Grandpa was just driving up with the others. All were horrified by her account of the accident. She didn't let on that it was Pam's fault, because what difference whose fault it was? The harm had been done. But she couldn't bear to look at Pam or speak to her.

She followed as Grandpa hurried to Challenger's stall. "You did right to use cold water," he said after examining him. "I don't think we need call the vet. I should know what to do after my years of experiences with sick and injured horses." He fetched the antitetanus bottle and hypodermic needle from his kit and gave Challenger a shot. This evening, he said, and for the next couple of days, Challenger's routine must be more hosing in half-hour periods, hand walking to keep up his circulation, and a light diet. No grain, only hay. Later, walking in the sea would be good. He thought the legs would heal all right, but not in time to show here. Challenger would have to be scratched from all his classes. Ellie wondered unhappily how this accident would affect his spirits. She knew that Grandpa, too, worried about this though he didn't say so. It would be

135

miserable having to wait for what would happen the first time Challenger was asked to jump.

That night and several times during the next few days Ellie remembered how she and Pam had agreed at the beach that Santa Barbara was so enjoyable and so leisurely. Things were different now. Besides her constant care and worry for Challenger, her usual work was keeping her on the run. Other exhibitors were arriving, offering all sorts of jobs. When they learned she wouldn't be showing Challenger, several of them asked her to show a horse in the hunter classes. At least she would earn something in place of what Challenger might have won.

Grandpa had turned over Billy's lessons to Ellie, for the Nelsons still took up a lot of his time. He had to spend time, too, with a brand new client. Everyone was delighted, Ellie probably most of all, because the new client owned the two jumpers which had been in Bull Johnson's care. It seemed Grandpa had had a few words with the show manager after Challenger's accident.

"A few words was all it took," Grandpa reported. "This manager knows me. He also knows Johnson and has received complaints before about the fellow. To make a long story short, he ordered Johnson off the grounds. I heard Johnson was swearing like a madman when his customer decided to stable his jumpers with us."

"Will I get to show them?" Ellie asked.

"No, they're too spooky for you to handle," Grandpa replied. "In any case, their owner doesn't want them shown until they put on some weight—a very sensible decision. Possibly I'll have you lead or longe them while I'm horse hunting with the Nelsons. And I'll have you go on with Billy's lessons. You've been successful with him as well as with Pamela. I believe you're developing a talent for teaching."

Ellie didn't answer. Challenger had been hurt only two days ago, and since then she hadn't spoken to Pam. Even at supper, even in bed, they ignored each other. Ellie just couldn't imagine having anything more to do with her, like riding lessons.

Grandpa must have noticed the strained silence in the trailer. "I can understand that you're disappointed in Pamela," he said. "You didn't say she was to blame but obviously the fault was hers, letting Johnson school Challenger. But I think you're being unfair. She doesn't know Johnson. She meant well. It was simply ignorance on her part."

Still Ellie said nothing, only blinked hard because she was close to tears. It was a good thing Grandpa didn't know she had called Pam a dope and wished she was dead and said, "I suppose you'd like to kill my horse!" His sharp blue eyes fixed on hers as if he saw into her mind. "Would you rather I took over her schooling?" he asked.

It was a tough question. Of course she would rather he did. But that would mean giving up her bargain about being his assistant if she trained Pam to do well in the medal. And he had just said she was developing a talent for teaching! She struggled to give some kind of answer and finally murmured, "I guess I could go on schooling her." All at once her throat filled with a lump and two tears squeezed from her eyes. Her voice choked. "Oh, but Grandpa, poor Challenger! He trusted us, and she wrecked him. Now he won't want to jump for ages, maybe never. I just know the confidence is all knocked out of him." Prospects which had looked discouraging suddenly looked hopeless. All those long patient months of restoring Challenger's trust were for nothing. Ellie shoved back her bangs with a desperate gesture. "I don't know what to do about Pam. I honestly don't."

"It's up to you, Ellen," Grandpa said quietly. "But Pamela's progress is up to me, since her parents are paying me for it. If you feel you can't continue with her, I'll replace you. But you must make up your mind, for I can't neglect her. Give me your answer tomorrow."

That night again there was silence in the trailer. Ellie

could hardly remember ever being so mixed up and miserable. She cried a little into her pillow and suspected from the sounds above her that Pam was crying too.

Next morning Challenger began his salt water cure. Ellie figured she was going to see enough beach in the next week to last her the rest of her life. Probably she would get a million new freckles. But it was worth anything to see Challenger walking nearly sound and standing while the water crept up over his feet to his poor scarred knees. At first he had lowered his head suspiciously to snort at this strange liquid advancing as if it were alive. It must have felt good, though, for he rapidly grew bolder until he was wading up to his belly. Soon he didn't want to come out at all! Ellie had rolled up her jeans to lead him in but soon found she should have worn her swim suit. The long rollers that crashed far out sent curling edges racing in to break against her and spray her with foam. She didn't care how wet or sunburned she got, or that her retainer tasted like dried seaweed. She wouldn't mind anything so long as Challenger returned to normal.

There was one good thing at least—he had forgiven her for his accident, if he ever blamed her. He treated her just as he always had, nuzzling at her hands and nickering to her. Now, in the water, he wanted to play together. Also he had forgiven Pam. Ellie knew this because she had seen them talking at his stall door. She had pretended not to notice that Pam stood whispering to him, extending one hand pleadingly. He had come forward to snuff her palm with velvet nostrils and it was really pretty darn nice the way they acted together. As Ellie watched him now while he pawed and splashed, she felt something like shame. He wasn't holding a grudge . . . She reflected, as often before, that many animals were finer than people. No matter what treatment they received, they forgave the humans who abused them. In his generous heart, Challenger held only love. . . . How come hers held resentment?

He had stopped playing and stood quietly, gazing out to sea. She leaned against his shoulders, roughened by sand and spray, and closed her eyes for a better smell of the ocean. "I'm mean," she said sadly, "mean and cruel to Pam." She opened her eyes and saw Challenger's head proudly raised, meeting the world with deep untroubled eyes in spite of all he had suffered.

Ellie too straightened and now her voice was firmer, her will steady. "You're going to quit being a rag doll and show some spirit," she told herself. "Go on, stupid, go make up with Pam this instant." Grasping Challenger's halter she ordered "March!" so loudly that he gave a startled bounce just as a wave rolled in. Ellie was drenched by a glorious blue-green shower that left her blinded and sputtering. No doubt amused by her plight, Challenger set off gaily for home, dragging her behind him.

"Oh, death!" she gasped, lunging and plunging through the deep sand. "Wait, Challenger, wait!" He was having too much fun, and wouldn't slow down till they reached the street and Ellie faced astonished passers-by. "You big clown," she panted. "I thought you were supposed to have sore legs!"

At the barn no one was in sight but, as she closed Challenger's stall door, the trailer door opened. Pam appeared, dressed in her street clothes. She was shoving and bumping her two big suitcases from the trailer.

"What on earth are you doing?" Ellie asked, too surprised to remember they weren't speaking.

Pam looked pale and sort of grim. She answered shortly. "I'm leaving."

"What!"

"I do not care to be the house guest of a person who called me a stupid dope and wished I was dead and accused me of trying to murder her horse."

Ellie realized only too well that she had been perfectly insulting. "Where are you going?" she said nervously.

"Home to Los Angeles," Pam replied. She tugged at her bags and slid them forward a fraction.

Suddenly Ellie was horrified at how cruel she had

been to Pam. She started to apologize and then couldn't help seeing the funny side of Pam's heroic struggles. Torn between remorse and amusement she managed to ask, "Just how were you planning to go?"

"Bus," Pam answered through clenched teeth, kicking the nearest suitcase, which jumped ahead an inch.

Ellie had an hysterical vision of her friend kicking and jerking her luggage downtown to the bus depot. The picture was too much for her strained nerves. In a desperate effort not to laugh she heard herself making sounds like a clucking hen.

Pam's face showed the weirdest mixture of indignation, bewilderment and—was that the beginning of a smile?

Ellie was overjoyed to see it but still cautious. "Would you mind telling me what you see that's funny?" she asked politely.

"You!" Pam cried, suddenly breaking into the old giggles. "You're dripping like a fish, hair plastered down, clothes stuck to you—what happened?"

Before Ellie described Challenger's playfulness, she sobered down and apologized for the way she had treated Pam. Then Pam apologized again for having hurt Challenger. How lucky, they agreed, that Ellie had come back in time to stop her going. And how ghastly it would have been if Grandpa had come back to find her gone!

As if their thought had called him, he came toward the trailer with the Nelsons and Bannisters. Naturally he noticed the girls' clothes. "Have you been to church?" he asked Pam. "Ellie, you've been swimming?"

"Uh—not exactly," Ellie stammered.

Then he saw the suitcases. "What are those doing there?"

"Those?" Pam echoed with apparent amazement as if she had just noticed them.

Ellie didn't dare look at her. She heard a strangled giggle when she too repeated, "Those?"

A pause followed while they all stared at the bags. Then Pam, purple in the face, said, "Oh, those," as if explaining everything. "They belong in the trailer," she added faintly.

"Then put them in the trailer," Grandpa ordered.

The girls hurried to obey. Pam was still trembling with smothered laughter, but Ellie felt only gratefulness for their narrow escape. They had been spared embarrassing explanations. Much more important, they had been saved from maybe losing each other for keeps. Never again, she resolved, would she risk tragedy by failing to say those two little words, "I'm sorry."

9. All Aboard

HOW impossible, Ellie thought several months later, that here she was the first week of November, headed for Madison Square Garden! How perfectly dreamy to be on a train with Challenger, and how marvelous of him to be taking the noise and motion so calmly. She herself was far from calm. She had been too excited to eat or sleep properly ever since the Mortons invited her and Challenger to go East with Pam and Flight. They had wanted to do this in return for her helping Pam win the medal at Santa Barbara. Tonight in Los Angeles Pam and Flight would board the train. And in two weeks the four of them would show in the medal finals!

Ellie looked up at Challenger from where she sat leaning against his wooden crate. It was almost too much to hope he would remain satisfied in it for four days, even with her close by. She would have to rub him, especially his legs, in place of exercise. Already she had to rub the seat of her pants as she scrambled to her feet. "These old boards get hard after four hours," she said. "And we still have four hours to go till Los Angeles. Then four days on the Santa Fe. We'll miss a lot of scenery in here with only little high windows. But don't worry, I won't leave you, except to eat and sleep. I'll even sleep here if you're nervous, or if Flight is, because I should look after her too, Grandpa said. Sharing a berth with Pam would have been a riot though. Who ever thought I'd be sleeping on a train, whizzing through the night past cities and farms and everything?"

She walked around cautiously in the dim rattling car, remembering how thrilling it had been to see Pam win her medal. Her win had been due mainly to the pure determination of them both. Pam had resolved to "show" everyone that she was smarter than she had looked at her first try; and of course she had been dying to hear the music of applause just for her. Ellie had been equally anxious to "show" Grandpa that she was capable of getting good results as a trainer. Then they had had help from an unexpected source. Anita Sherlock had turned up, the most glamorous actress of all, according to Pam. Pam had managed to be introduced to her, and Miss Sherlock was very kind, and described the famous School of Drama in New York. Pam declared she would die unless she got to visit it. She simply had to win the medal and go to New York. Miss Sherlock had given her an entirely new impression of acting as a career. For the first time Pam realized it would take a lot of hard, tedious, patient work. To Ellie's surprise, that prospect didn't in the least discourage Pam.

"You're like my parents," Pam had said. "They don't take my ambition seriously. They don't believe I'd be willing to work at it."

"Because, let's face it, you've never really worked at anything," Ellie had answered. It was swell how completely frank and friendly they had grown, more so since they had been enemies over Challenger's accident.

"I guess that's it," Pam admitted. "They have the same opinion of my riding. So now I'll have to do extra well in the finals, to prove I can be hard working and serious about whatever I take up."

"And don't forget I'll help you," Ellie answered. "Just like together we corrected the way you were sitting back too soon. See, I know you so well—that is, your style of riding—that it's easy to . . . Oh, I can't explain exactly, but when I watch you ride it's as if it was me I saw, my hands and my brain and everything. You know what I mean?" Pam nodded, and Ellie went on. "I half wish I wasn't in the finals, too, so I could give you even more help."

"Then stay out," Pam said smiling, "and maybe I'll have a chance to win."

Howard Prescott was to judge again at the Garden. He was a nice person, Ellie thought. She and Grandpa had met him after she had won the medal, and he had complimented Grandpa on having "an outstanding pupil." His congratulations had gone on until from embarrassment Ellie had blushed and nearly swallowed her retainer.

In the half light of the baggage car she spread out Challenger's blanket and lay down on it, resting her head against her canvas bag. This bag held her second best clothes. Her best were in a borrowed suitcase. Her stable tools and tack would fit into Pam's elegant tack trunk tonight.

How the family had rushed around making preparations till the very last minute, washing, mending, ironing, and adding to her wardrobe from her sisters'! All of them had loaned her some savings from baby sitting and other jobs so she would have spending money. With almost no regret she had even auctioned off her collection of stuffed animals to the seventh grade. And such debates there had been over the proposed journey, and over missing school, while letters flew back and forth between Sayres and Mortons. Ellie knew this trip would never have been allowed except that Jim and Dolly

Nelson offered to go too. They said they hadn't had a real honeymoon and this would be it. Also they would see Dolly's family, who lived in New York. With them for chaperones all parents were satisfied.

Ellie dozed a couple of hours, aware of her head bouncing and body jolting in uneasy rest. Now and then she opened her eyes, to see Challenger dozing too, his head over the front of the crate. He didn't want food or drink, although she offered him water in his own bucket whenever they stopped long enough to fill it at some station. According to Grandpa, one should be suspicious of strange buckets, strange tools and strangers themselves unless they were sufficiently bowlegged to prove themselves horsemen! So, in the baggage car, Ellie and Challenger drifted between waking and sleeping until the train moved slowly into the big city. With a final groan and grind it stopped at last, while porters yelled, "Los Angeles! Union Station, Los Angeles!"

A little nervous, Ellie stood at Challenger's head with a firm grasp of his halter in case he got panicky. She didn't know what to do with a panicky horse who might start to kick and struggle in his crate. She could only wait, and hope he would be all right, and wish for Pam and Flight.

She remembered to roll open her car door, then darted

back to Challenger. Above the station noise Pam's voice called, "Where are they?" Then someone on the platform shouted, "In there, folks. Right there."

For a second Ellie forgot Challenger and rushed to the door, calling, "Pam! Hey Pam, here we are!"

Next, Challenger neighed, sensing his friend's approach, and Flight answered with a sort of hysterical whinny. Good grief, was she going to give trouble? She was led by the Mortons' groom, and she looked pretty wild-eyed. Pam hovered close and the Nelsons stayed a safe distance away.

The girls waved to each other, but distractedly. They didn't try to talk during the business of loading Flight into the car and then into her crate opposite Challenger's. Plainly the crate made her nervous. She pushed forward, then backed up, tossed her head, switched her tail. Little by little, though, she seemed to abandon the notion of trying to climb out. By the time her groom left and Ellie clanged the car door shut Flight only pawed occasionally and kept her eyes on Challenger as if he gave her courage.

On their way at last, Pam and Ellie turned eagerly to see each other. Questions and answers and exclamations flew back and forth. As Flight gradually became less nervous, the girls too began to relax. Ellie was able to admire Pam's outfit, a smart tweed traveling suit with a perky hat and matching pumps and bag.

"You couldn't be more unsuitably dressed for the baggage car," Ellie chuckled.

"I'll go back and change into jodhpurs when we stop," Pam said. "The Nelsons have my bags." She laughed. "Didn't they look startled that I was traveling in here? But they're darlings, perfect for chaperones. The crabbiest thing she ever says is, 'Oh, I don't think . . .' and then she'll let you do anything. Jim's just as nice. They even look alike, have you noticed?"

"Yes, both real fair," Ellie agreed. "She's so cute, no wonder she's called Dolly. And he's sort of cute too, his round face and crew cut and all."

"They won't give us any trouble," Pam said mischievously. "Only they made me promise we'd eat dinner with them."

That bothered Ellie. "You can," she said. "I'll have to stay here unless the horses act completely quiet. After all, I'm supposed to take care of them. You can smuggle me a bone or something. And most likely I better sleep here tonight."

"Dolly'll have a fit," Pam said. "And the conductor probably won't let you."

As night approached, Ellie was pleased to see that

both horses kept falling asleep. The rhythmic clackety-clack of wheels on rails seemed to soothe them. Ellie studied her marked map by flashlight and decided she could take time off for dinner. The train would stop at Barstow and they could make a dash for the dining car. Before they stopped again an hour or so later, she could settle on plans for the night.

When the train slowed for Barstow she filled the hay nets sparingly as Grandpa had ordered from the bales he had sent. He had also advised no grain but plenty of water. Both horses were drowsily munching when the girls left their car.

In the Pullman the Nelsons were waiting anxiously. The four of them had a section. Pam begged for the lower berth because of the window. After a visit to the dressing room, she and Ellie followed the others to the dining car. What fun it was to sit there cosily and have delicious food served with a flourish by smiling colored waiters. Amazing, thought Ellie, how the waiters carried huge loaded trays without losing their balance, and set down full cups or bowls without spilling a drop. She and Pam had to giggle at the poor lady across the aisle who was trying to spoon cereal into a balky baby. Between the motion of the train and the baby's acrobatics the cereal went everywhere except into its mouth.

Watching with fascination, the girls only controlled their laughter when Dolly said gently, "I don't think. . ."

"Of course you don't," Jim cut in. "You just sit and be pretty and I'll do the thinking in this family."

In spite of the good food and fun, Ellie kept worrying about the horses. Around eight o'clock she was able to check on them. Both were contented. In fact Challenger seemed a little indignant that he was disturbed after he had settled down to sleep. But Ellie couldn't bear to leave them standing all night in manure. With her shovel she removed their droppings, which she dumped into a basket brought for that purpose. Just how she would empty the basket she hadn't yet decided. Following Grandpa's orders she blanketed the horses, checked and rechecked to make sure they were safe and secure. She was considering whether to borrow more blankets from her berth and sleep here when Pam arrived breathless with a message from Dolly. Dolly begged Ellie to come back to the section. She said it would be dreadful to sleep in a baggage car. Pam hadn't put up much of an argument beyond "Oh well," and Ellie too gave in, since it didn't really seem necessary for her to stay with the horses.

She and Pam had a grand time in their lower berth beneath the shiny brown underside of the upper. There was still so much that had happened in the past two months to talk over that they gossiped for nearly two hours. The green curtains enclosing them kept them private, yet they could hear and secretly laugh at conversations near by. All around them were the rattles and creaks and mysterious iron bangings of the train, and occasionally the lonesome wail of the whistle. After a while they snapped off the bedside light and pushed up their blind. At first the world rushing past looked all black. As their eyes adjusted they were able now and then to make out a town or fields and trees. Once they crossed a river, where the train made a metallic clatter on the bridge. When they shot into a tunnel Pam laughed as Ellie jumped back from the window. While the train rushed through the tunnel, everything smelled sooty. Once they tore by a solitary house where a light burned, maybe for a sick person, they thought, or a woman alone waiting up for her husband. And then Ellie was certain she glimpsed a group of horses in a pasture, their heads raised to watch the train roaring past like a dragon in the night. Conversation returned to their own horses, until no other sounds came from beyond their curtain, except an occasional muffled cough or broken words spoken in sleep. The Santa Fe at last rocked the girls unconscious, still talking.

All next day in the baggage car, when they could

sneak past Dolly and the conductor, they talked about the big show ahead. Several times they said, "I wonder how we'll feel two weeks from now, coming home—happy or sad?" Then there were so many questions about the Garden: How big was it, how tough would competition be, how scared would they be, and so on. New York itself was thrilling just to think about.

Sitting on blankets near the horses the second day out, Ellie and Pam drifted into serious discussion of the future. After Pam outlined again her plan to study drama, Ellie again described how she had been assisting

Grandpa after school and weekends. With that start, she was more than ever determined to become a successful trainer.

"By the time I'm through high school," she said, "Grandpa will need me full time. He isn't getting any younger. I wonder how he's doing without me." She missed him, his rules and his fussiness and his wise or weird sayings.

"He's young enough to fall for Mrs. Bannister, she hopes," Pam pointed out. She grinned. "Of course he'd like her better if she pretended to be a little bowlegged."

Ellie shook her head. "No. He'd guess, and think she was dishonest. Besides, it's just about impossible to pretend you're bowlegged. I know because I've tried," she admitted. "But at least their being friendly gives me a chance with Billy. He does fine when I coach him, better than with Grandpa, if I do say so. See, he's scared of Grandpa, but I kind of kid him along till he's doing things he really doesn't like, only I make him think he likes them."

"Psychology, that's called," Pam said. "All good teachers are supposed to have it. It helps them handle people in real foxy ways."

Ellie laughed. "Sounds sort of sneaky." She looked up at Challenger, who was watching Flight as if they too were enjoying a good gossip. "Isn't he beautiful?"

she murmured. "So big and muscled. And smart. He thinks, you know, just like people. He's sure improved a lot these last months. If he could just do well in New York it would be the best thing for him. He's got the kind of character that needs to feel important, like he's really a success. Failure makes him feel guilty."

Pam was looking at his knees. "Thank heavens they're all right," she said. "I would never ever forgive myself if I'd wrecked him for keeps." Her big brown eyes showed remorse even at the thought.

"Well, you didn't," Ellie answered, "and he took to jumping again without any fuss, like a good sport." She lay back on the blankets and returned to the subject of training. "It's terribly interesting how you'll see something that's wrong in a horse or rider, and you try and try to figure what's the reason for it. Like solving a math problem. And finally when you get it, wow, you feel good, though lots of times it's some simple little thing that was making the trouble. And it's good to get folks interested in riding as a hobby. It makes them healthy and relaxed and carefree. And it helps their character, Grandpa says, because they have to develop patience and self-control and reasoning." She didn't mention, because it sounded impolite, that she thought the summer's efforts had improved Pam's character. Instead she said, "Helping other riders has sure been good for me.

Golly, when I coach people I'm the one who needs patience and all that stuff." She sighed, thinking how much she lacked those qualities. Then she sat up and reached into her hip pocket for the rule book. "Ready for a quiz?" she suggested.

Pam ignored the suggestion. "Since you're such a brain," she said slyly, "I suppose you've figured what to do with the manure basket."

"Naturally," said Ellie. "As a matter of fact I figured two choices of what to do with it."

"A genius," Pam murmured.

"Either (a) we arrive in New York with it full, and—uh—present it to the station master. Or (b) we open this door at dead of night and empty it into space."

"Don't you dare open the door while we're moving," Pam warned. "We'd fall out sure. And I don't believe the station master would appreciate your little gift. No, put your mind to work again."

"Meantime, put yours to work and study the rule book," Ellie ordered. "I can see perfectly well you're only trying to distract me from quizzing you." She chuckled. "That's another thing I've learned from teaching. People get you to talking when they want to dodge work."

She herself hadn't dodged any care of her charges on this journey. Of course it was always a pleasure to groom Challenger. He loved being brushed and sponged and polished, especially if Ellie kept talking to him. He didn't object, like so many horses, to having his mane and tail combed. In these few days he had learned to appreciate having his legs massaged in place of exercise. He would breathe long contented sighs when Ellie rubbed from his shoulder or rump down to his hoofs. Altogether, she thought as she surveyed him critically, he probably hadn't lost more than a few pounds, which was natural for a horse when traveling.

She wasn't as satisfied with Flight. The mare had never quite settled down. She fidgeted and fussed, the train made her nervous. More and more she laid back her ears and reached as if to nip. Attentions only annoyed her. Maybe the noise bothered her, or the constant movement. At any rate she wasn't eating or drinking enough. Probably she had lost seventy to a hundred pounds. That wasn't an awful lot for a horse; still, the third day out, Ellie decided it was lucky only one day's traveling remained.

With Jim Nelson's help she had solved the manure basket problem by tipping a porter to empty it during a night stop. Now only this one night was left, and it was more and more exciting to imagine arriving, being met by a man from the Garden with a van. Ellie knew Challenger sensed he was nearing a new place. Maybe the change in weather told him, for days were brisk and each night was colder. The last dinner on the train was like a party, with the Nelsons almost as thrilled as Pam and Ellie at the prospect of seeing New York, especially the Garden.

Days and weeks later, when Ellie thought of her carelessness that night, she still couldn't understand or explain it. She knew she would remember it always. There was no excuse for it, or maybe the only little bit of excuse was the excitement that took her mind from her chores. Pam couldn't share the blame, because Ellie had gone alone to settle the horses for the night. The train was stopping only ten minutes, so she was hurrying, but this didn't excuse her either. It wasn't till next morning at the station in New York that she found she had forgotten to blanket Flight.

Even Pam could tell the mare was sick. Her eyes were dull, her nostrils dry and her head drooped. "She's caught cold," Pam said in a small voice. Her tone gave it away that she was trying to hide her dismay.

The man who had brought the van was blunter. "Looks to me like pneumonia," he said.

The Nelsons said consoling things, to which no one listened.

Ellie alone was too stunned to say anything at all.

10. The Garden

IT was a dismal group that surrounded poor Flight in the baggage car, amidst the racket and confusion of the huge New York station. Ellie was fighting tears of shame while she blanketed the mare, now—too late—instead of last night. The thought that Flight might have pneumonia almost made her sick herself. She was too wretched to know quite what she was doing, and she was grateful to leave all arrangements to the man who had brought the van.

Man or boy? she wondered distractedly. His blunt face, lively gray eyes, and curly black hair with no hat looked about thirty years old. Yet he was so active and chatty that he seemed young, and so did his black turtle-necked sweater. Also he was pretty fresh, calling her "Freckles" and Pam "Sweetheart" before he had known them five minutes. But at the moment he was such a life saver that no one objected to his manners.

"Andy's the name," he announced. "Handy Andy, they call me," and he winked at Pam, who blushed at such familiarity. Undiscouraged, he turned to Jim, after showing his identification papers. "Guess you know Mr. Morton wrote the Garden to send me. Told them he wanted a responsible character to look after the girlies and their horses. So here I am, most responsible character in all New York, and aren't they the lucky ones?"

The only answer was a murmur from Dolly, "Oh, I don't think . . ."

"Best thing we can do with her," he continued, jerking a thumb toward Flight, "is get her indoors quick and call the vet. Doc Fowler's at the Garden, he's a good 'un."

While he talked he was gathering up the horses' belongings, moving swiftly. The shovel, buckets and haynets, broom and pitchfork he piled in the famous manure basket, now empty. Then he haltered both horses and snapped on their lead ropes. He whistled for a porter and directed him to remove the baggage on his handcart. He did this so briskly that Jim's only job was to bring the tack trunk.

A few minutes later they were leading the horses

through staring crowds to the street where Andy had parked. There the Nelsons left by cab for the Sportsman's Hotel, with all the luggage except stable things. Ellie thought it odd of them not to come straight to the Garden. But as Dolly said, they knew so little about horses that they would be more nuisance than help. It was more practical for them to check in at the hotel and unpack for all four.

The cold gray morning matched Ellie's mood. She tightened the plaid mackinaw which had been her folks' parting present. Pam had one like it, snugly lined, only hers had a small round fur collar which was very becoming. On the way to the Garden they sat with Andy in the front of the van. Luckily for Flight it was a closed one. The girls were silent from a mixture of wonder at these new surroundings and depression over Flight. Ellie knew both were dreading the same thing: must the mare be scratched from showing? Through their silence Andy talked enough for three, pointing out famous landmarks and buildings that streaked up to dizzy heights. His driving, through the heavy traffic, had a dashing style that was breathtaking.

Worry about Flight was so awful Ellie couldn't stand it. For distraction she asked Andy about the Sportsman's Hotel. It was on Fifty-fifth Street, he said, six blocks from the Garden.

"Crummy old joint, them potted palms in the lobby, and red velvet drapes like you'd expect in a doggone museum. But it's handy, and they're used to horsemen. Everyone with the show stays there. Their restaurant's open all hours. Nice little bar too," he added as if the girls were likely to be having cocktails.

During the drive Ellie grew accustomed to the jerky way he spoke. She was wondering just how much of his time and help the Mortons had arranged for, when he answered her thought.

"I got bad news for you. You'll have to share me with a couple other exhibitors. But don't worry, you can count on Handy Andy when you need him." And somehow, in spite of his funny manner, that was exactly the impression he gave, that he would be dependable. Certainly one small-town girl was more than thankful for his guidance. Ellie didn't know how New York compared with Los Angeles, but it sure made South San Francisco seem like a village. Even Grandpa might have been a bit stunned by this tremendous city, its skyscrapers and rivers of traffic and millions of people. She wished with all her heart that he were here now so that he, instead of strangers, could advise her about Flight.

Fortunately Challenger was no problem. He unloaded calmly in front of the great building, and even posed before walking in, to let passers-by admire him. Since his body was blanketed and his legs were wrapped the people couldn't see much. Ellie hadn't taken any chances of his white stockings getting scratched during his travels. She stepped back so as not to hide him when several people stopped to stare at the big horse with the fine neck and noble head. In turn he watched Flight. To Ellie his wise eyes plainly showed concern for his friend and stable mate. Oh death, she thought, let's not have him depressed, too.

The Garden was humming with confusion, but it was the kind of show-time confusion that Ellie understood. To her it was what they called background music—joyful music ordinarily, but not today. Her guilty conscience spoiled everything. They paused just inside to avoid being trampled. "Would you toss me on?" she asked Andy, and she crooked her left knee for a leg-up.

"With no bridle?" he said, cocking his head doubtfully.

"Oh, sure. He'll follow Flight," she said, knowing the rope and halter were all she needed for control. In the mob of horsemen, some riding, some leading, she felt safer mounted than afoot. It struck her as surprising that so many had arrived this soon. Everyone must be seeking the same advantage, a chance to get used to the ring before showing.

Evidently Andy had already located their stalls, for

he led the way down a ramp that brought them to the basement. Here were the stables, rows and rows of stalls as in a riding school. The air was close, with a lovely smell of animals and feed, liniment and leather. Clearly, no matter how strict the management was about cleanliness, an underground stable couldn't have the freshness of an outdoor one. Ellie noticed that Challenger kept snuffing, testing this peculiar place not only with eyes and ears but with his nostrils. Luckily he was curious rather than alarmed. How different from the old Challenger, who would have flinched at every shout or bang!

Flight moved in a daze with lowered head and listless eyes. She seemed unaware of Pam and Andy on either side of her. She didn't step aside for anyone and could have been kicked or bumped except that Andy made way for her with warnings of "Heads up!" or "Coming through." Once he stopped to avoid running down a small boy who wavered in the middle of the aisle. Andy stooped and spoke with surprising gentleness. "Lost, son? Better stand over there, against the wall." And he waited to see the child safely aside before he led his group on.

Ellie felt a bit shabby in her jeans and old shoes, with no hat. Of course there were no Western classes here, therefore no Western clothes. Some of the people evidently were gaited riders, elegant in slim tapering pants, belled at the ankle. Some, Ellie could guess, had ponies or hacknies or fine harness horses. Most wore britches or jodhpurs, and tweed jackets in contrast to her mackinaw. It would be all the better for her career if the trainers were mostly connected with hunters. She should be able to learn a lot from them. She wondered if she could ask all the questions she wanted without having been introduced. If not, who would introduce her? The only person she would know here was the judge, Howard Prescott, and he might have forgotten her. That seemed unlikely after the long talk he'd had with her and Grandpa following her win at Palm Springs. But you didn't act chummy with a judge, no matter how well you knew him. If you did and then you won, the gossips accused you of making up to him, and they accused him of favoring you.

At the stalls Andy left the girls. "You settle your horses while I go for Doc Fowler. And I'll fetch your tack box and stuff. Don't let the mare eat or drink or lie down." He must be thinking that Flight could have colic. It always struck Ellie as odd that a horse with a stomach ache must be kept on its feet, not at all like people. "There's no exercise in lying down," Grandpa had explained. "Exercise is what they need to put their plumbing to work."

"It's a pretty small stall," she grumbled, closing Challenger in. He agreed by giving her such a reproachful look that she lingered to pat him and whisper. "Never mind, honey. You'll be all right." She hurried next door to tie Flight while Pam watched sadly, her thoughts plain to guess. Ellie wanted desperately to say something consoling, but what was there to say? Only that she was horribly, horribly ashamed to have caused Flight's sickness. But for once no apology would help, and to mention what both dreaded, having to scratch Flight, might make them both cry.

Familiar with the routine of settling in, Ellie signaled the feed man on his rounds and ordered according to Grandpa's instructions—a sack of rolled oats, one of bran and two bales of timothy hay. In New York, it seemed, they used timothy instead of oat hay.

It was past noon when Doc Fowler appeared. He was a tall old gentleman with, of all things, a droopy white mustache which kept reminding Ellie of a walrus. But she was in no mood to smile as she watched him approach his patient. No doubt from experience with ill-tempered ones he soothed Flight with hands and voice before he examined her. He needn't have worried. She stood limp while he took her temperature then felt the pulse under her throat, counting the beats with eyes on his wrist watch. He made sure from Pam that Flight had been given distemper and sleeping sickness shots, and inquired about her usual habits and behavior.

Ages went by before he gave his verdict: bronchitis. With proper care she would be all right. "But," he instructed Pam, "don't take any chances. Keep her warm. Very light feed. Plenty of water. Above all, rest. Don't even take her out of the stall until I check on her again. I'll give her a shot of penicillin." He produced the hypodermic from his bag and some capsules which he handed

Pam. Pam didn't know how to make Flight swallow them, but Ellie did. All it took was vaseline to grease the fingers and a bold hand to slip them well back in a horse's mouth.

Now the doctor was preparing to leave, without having mentioned Flight's showing next week. Pam thanked him in a small voice. There was a pause while she struggled to ask the fatal question. She just couldn't make herself do it, Ellie saw. And no wonder. Until the words were actually said—"You must scratch Flight"— there was hope. At least they could pretend to hope.

Doc Fowler was going, and still Pam remained silent. Ellie took a step forward. Her voice too was small and kind of shaky as she said, "Will she—I mean, will the mare have to be scratched from the show?"

The doctor turned back. His walrus mustache quivered as if with surprise at such a question. "Definitely," he said, and walked away.

Then Pam did the bravest thing. With tears in her eyes she shrugged and said, "Oh, well." As if it didn't matter at all!

Ellie knew at once what she must do. They stood close together outside the stalls where Flight breathed heavily and Challenger was mumbling for attention. This once Ellie ignored him. For a minute, while her plan formed, she stood only half aware of her surroundings. From other aisles came whistling, the sounds of hammering and faucets running, and of horses pawing, neighing, chewing. Somewhere one squealed, and from its thin voice it must have been a Shetland pony. Ellie wondered if her own voice would sound ordinary enough. It was funny how sounds were magnified and echoed in the forest of cement and steel pillars that supported the ring above. Preparing to speak, she licked her lips and found they tasted of tanbark. She could smell the tanbark even way down here. This basement was kind of like a tomb, at least it had become the tomb of her high hopes to win the finals.

Ellie realized that now it was her turn to put on an act. She remembered how sorry Pam had been for having caused Challenger's accident at Santa Barbara, and how meanly she herself had treated Pam. Now their positions were reversed. She was the one responsible for Flight's trouble. Instead of acting nasty, Pam had already forgiven her. Yet this time the situation was much more serious. In Challenger's case, he had had to be scratched only from unimportant classes, since he had already won his medal. Here Pam would miss the finals, after three thousand miles of traveling and goodness knows what expense and plans and arrangements.

Ellie knew she wasn't much of an actress. But if Pam could pretend not to care, with a mere "Oh, well," then she could do the same. In fact, it was the very least she could do to pay for her forgetfulness. She would have to be foxy about this plot though or it would fail.

She pocketed her hands, which had been nervously twisting her bangs. "I guess I'll go to the office," she said casually as possible. "There might be some mail for us. And—oh, while I'm there, shouldn't I see about scratching Flight?"

"Maybe I better do it," Pam answered.

That was exactly what Ellie wanted to prevent. Yet she didn't dare insist on going, for fear Pam would get suspicious.

"Why don't you wait here?" she suggested. "I'm more used to that kind of business. I'll be right back." She started away as if the matter was settled. Hearing no answer, she looked back to see Pam lower her face into both hands while tears shone between her curtains of brown hair. Ellie hurried off. She had to blink hard and swallow a big lump. "It's got to work," she muttered.

Upstairs, after taking a couple of wrong turns, she found the horse show office. One of the turns had led to an entrance where she had a sudden view of the ring. In fascination she stood staring at the beautiful carpet of rich red tanbark where so many dreams would shatter or come true. An alley surrounded it, separating it from the box seats. Back of those rose tier after tier of bleachers.

She pictured them full of people, thousands of faces, thousands of eyes all following the hunter who proudly performed over the fences. Big and stout fences they were, but easy for him. She could practically hear the applause like thunder. And she could see this horse—a dazzling chestnut whose foretop rose and fell over a white diamond. Inside him there was a kind of song that only his rider could hear. . . . With a long sigh she turned away.

The office, like all horse show offices, was buzzing with arguments, greetings, complaints and ringing telephones. Ellie stood waiting her turn to speak. It was like waiting at the dentist, only a hundred times worse. She wanted her turn to hurry and come, yet it came much too fast. A woman clerk snapped at her, "You're next."

"It's about the medal finals, hunt seat," she said. "I have to scratch out."

As if she couldn't care less, the clerk said, "Name?" She was checking her list of entries.

"Ellen Sayre."

"Oh, yes." One little pencil mark crossed out the most exciting prospect in the world.

"About the horse—" Ellie began.

The clerk cut in briskly. "You should know that only riders, not horses, are entered in equitation classes."

Ellie nodded. That made her business easier, much easier than she had expected.

But the clerk didn't leave it at that. No doubt a lot of children came in here with all sorts of mixed-up ideas. "You should also know the entries have closed," the clerk said. "If you scratch you can't come back tomorrow and say you've changed your mind."

It helped Ellie's spirits to tell herself this clerk was a mean old thing. Still she didn't feel cheerful enough to discuss it all with Pam. Tonight would be soon enough. Pam would argue even though it was too late, and Ellie couldn't have stood that right now.

Walking slowly downstairs again she decided all at once she was tired and hungry. And cross. It must be midafternoon. Since the horses wouldn't need her and Pam for a while, they had better join the Nelsons at the hotel. Dolly and Jim must be getting worried. And then, someone would have to write the Mortons and Grandpa about Flight. She preferred not to picture Grandpa receiving the news. At least he would approve of the way she had handled the business in the office.

Andy had stopped by, Pam reported. He had said he could be reached in Aisle Five, where he was helping with the Worthington hackneys. With a rather strained smile she quoted him: " 'You need me any time, Sweetheart, holler.' " He slept in the Worthingtons' tack room and he would be back and forth during the night to keep an eye on Flight.

While Pam fussed over Flight, Ellie went in with Challenger so that he wouldn't feel neglected. Talking privately, she shook up his bedding, filled his bucket and blanketed him for the night. It was a little early to feed, but she knew he was hungry. He kept nudging her, then searching the corners where his feed pan should be. At last she gave in. But before she fed him she had Pam lead him while she cleaned his stall. As things were turning out it was lucky those two liked each other. Now they would have to become even closer friends. But not closer than she, Ellie herself, was to Challenger. That would be —well, after all, Challenger was hers. While he ate she swept the aisle in front of the three stalls, checked both latches and put away her tools in the third stall, which tomorrow they would fix for a tack room. After a final look at Flight she and Pam left for the hotel, a walk of six blocks according to Andy.

On the crowded sidewalks they kept bumping into people, because the girls were staring up at the tall buildings. By the time they reached the revolving doors of the old-fashioned hotel their necks ached. Their legs too were tired of trying to keep pace with the other pedestrians. Everyone seemed to be in a hurry. One man was pretty rude when Pam accidentally jostled him. To her breathless "I'm sorry" he growled something about "hicks from the sticks." "Well, my goodness, I said I was sorry!" Pam protested.

The Sportsman was much as Andy had described it—velvet drapes, potted palms, comfortably filled with horsemen.

"You'd know they were horsemen even without their clothes," Ellie whispered, as she and Pam crossed the lobby.

"Without their clothes—why, Ellen Sayre!" Pam whispered back, stifling a giggle.

Everything about the hotel delighted them. The man behind the desk who gave them their key looked properly sporty, and the "boy" who ran the elevator looked about a hundred years old. When he clanged open the door on the twenty-seventh floor, a dizzy view of the city from the hall window dazzled them. Their room too was exciting, with a thick carpet and a chandelier, and the beds covered with great puffy quilts.

After all they had been through, they were as glad to see the Nelsons as the Nelsons were to see them. To Ellie it was amazing that Jim and Dolly weren't more upset about Flight. The only excuse for them, as far as she could see, was that they were so absorbed in each other.

"Hicks from the sticks," Ellie repeated later, collapsing on the bed she had won by flipping to see who would sleep near the window.

Now Ellie's excitement was giving way to nervousness because she could no longer put off telling Pam what she had done in the horse show office. The only reason she hadn't told her before was that she just plain couldn't bear to talk about it. For a while she had almost managed to forget it, for the Nelsons avoided useless discussion of Flight or the finals. Tomorrow, they said, would be time enough to talk it all over. Tonight the girls should have fun.

The last two hours had indeed been fun. They had explored the Nelsons' room, phoned them just for laughs, bathed in the connecting bathroom, which had a lovely tub, and changed into dresses for dinner downstairs. But all the time Ellie was feeling sneaky for keeping her secret. It was a relief to be alone at last with Pam in their twin beds, to turn out the light and open the window on the roar of New York at night.

Any other time Ellie would have been thrilled just to lie there, hearing the city's giant voice, watching its lights reflected on the ceiling. Now she was concentrating wholly on how to break the news. The right words didn't come. Well, then, she would use any old words and get it over with. "Pam," she said abruptly, "in the horse show office today I canceled my name from the entries."

"*Your* name?"

"Yes."

There was a commotion in the other bed. "But—but El, Challenger's all right!" Pam sounded stunned.

"Of course he is. He'll show. And you know what? It's up to you to have him win."

"Up to me!" Pam cried, and now agitated rustling suggested she was getting up.

"Yes, up to you," Ellie repeated, "because you'll be on him."

A crash came from between the beds. Pam must have reached to turn on the lamp and knocked it over. Ellie was glad to have no light. Her face must look funny, as if she was going to cry. She was thinking of Challenger and what winning would mean to him. Her voice too was funny as she said, "Remember, he has a proud name . . ." She hadn't meant to stop there, but all at once talking had become impossible. It was bad enough having to listen to Pam's arguments which went on and on.

When Ellie couldn't stand any more she turned on her face, pulled the pillow over her head and mumbled, "Let's shut up now. Good night."

11. Sacrifice

ELLIE woke next morning from a dream of Grandpa. He was humming "Farewell, Shamrock Shores" so mournfully that she knew he was pleased. As she shook off the dream she thought grimly that he would be anything but pleased if he knew what was happening to his pupils. That reminded her that she must write and tell him today. No matter what he thought, neither he nor anyone could change her plans. Pam had seen that last night, even while babbling away about canceling herself.

Ellie rehearsed what she would say when Pam re-opened the argument, which was sure to happen. The rules were definite: Ellie could not get in again. If Pam scratched they would both be afoot. The worst part was, Challenger would miss showing in Madison Square Garden.

The very thought made Ellie sit up in the half-dark.

"You think I'd let him miss the biggest thrill of his whole life?" she said indignantly. "Why, he's probably the only horse in history to come all the way from California with a chance to beat the best horses in the East! And after spending two years to get where he is now, proud and confident instead of scared to death. What do you think it would do to his spirits if he had to just turn around and go home? He'd never trust me again!" She was stirring herself up by the words and gestures to finish loudly, "You're crazy."

"Thanks," Pam's sleepy voice came from the other bed. "But I give up," she added quickly. "Don't go on about it. It's a mess and all that, but I have to agree there's no point in our both scratching. Only, won't you at least try to get back in? Maybe there's some way . . . I know you're dying to show. It isn't fair."

"Now don't start that again," Ellie said. "We have work to do, so let's get up." The dressing table mirror reflected her long legs stepping from bed, her bangs on end and the metal gleam on her teeth.

It showed Pam propped on one smooth arm. Still pink from sleep, her face became solemn. "El, it's really Challenger you want to have win, isn't it?" she said. "I mean really. Not me, or you, but him."

"Of course," Ellie answered, padding over to close the window. "It would mean so much to him."

Behind her Pam said, "I wonder if it would."

For a moment Ellie stared down at the street, then turned back to sit on Pam's bed.

"Challenger needs success," she explained, frowning at Pam to make her understand. "If he won here he'd be the proudest horse in America. Just think, a bunch of nerves like he was, becoming champion! Of course you'd be proud too, as his rider. It would show your folks how determined you can be, so they'd know you'd really work at your drama. And it would be swell for me, having trained Challenger and partly trained you. And Grandpa would be tickled with such a good ad for his teaching. But if we don't do well, we'd get over being disappointed. Losing wouldn't absolutely wreck us because we don't have to prove we can make a comeback. For Challenger it's different. He needs to win."

It struck Ellie then that action rather than talk might help toward winning. "Let's get dressed and go," she said, reaching for her clothes.

"Without breakfast?"

"Sure without breakfast. Without washing too, or we'll wake the Nelsons. We can do all that later. Come on, hurry up. Handy Andy'll think we can't even care for our own horses."

"If he's so handy, let him do it," Pam grumbled, sounding for a minute like her old worst self. Ellie forgave her, knowing she didn't really mean it. Pam couldn't help hating to get up in the morning. You had to make allowance for people's weakness if you were going to understand them as well as horses. A good trainer must understand both—separately and together. Together was the hard part. Pam alone or Challenger alone would be a lot easier to handle than Pam on Challenger.

That fact grew clearer to Ellie this day and in the days which followed. She could scarcely remember ever having worked so hard. Leaving the hotel in the gray dawns, there was the long hike to the Garden. Then feeding, cleaning, grooming, schooling. There were trainers to question and watch after Andy had introduced her around. There were tack and tools to clean, the aisle to sweep, pans and buckets to scour. Then came the next round of feeding, cleaning, and bedding down. Flight took a lot of care too. Now that she had improved enough for exercise she had to be led during what seemed hours and miles. On top of this Ellie had arranged with Andy's help to do odd jobs for other exhibitors. She wanted to pay her expenses as much a possible rather than let the Mortons treat her to everything.

Not only physically but mentally she was under pressure. Since the scheme of having Pam show in her place had been hers, she desperately wanted it to succeed, most of all, naturally, for Challenger. The Nelsons didn't quite agree with it, but couldn't suggest any other plan. Actually they were so busy enjoying each other and Dolly's family that they saw very little of the girls. The Mortons wrote that they would never have allowed Ellie to make such a sacrifice, but they understood it was now too late to change. Grandpa answered Ellie's letter by airmail. It was a big relief to her that he and her folks approved. Several times during the hectic week she felt as if he were with her, at least in spirit. Picturing him and remembering his ways and words made the bad moments less discouraging and the good ones more satisfying.

During the first part of the week it seemed that nearly all times were bad. There was the day Challenger mysteriously acted panicky. Something or someone must have scared him, unknown to Ellie. Terrified that he might not get over it, she had to take a whole day from Pam's schooling to ride him herself, using all the tricks she knew until finally he calmed down. There was the day Pam did everything wrong, including falling off. For Ellie, there was a hardship she had never faced before—sore legs. From walking and running all day on cement, her calves ached painfully.

To add to the strain, both she and Pam were short of sleep. Their bedtime grew later and later because Ellie insisted they study their books and charts till they could hardly keep their eyes open. Propped up in bed, with yawns, nods and aching muscles, they took to drinking strong tea to stay awake. Without telling the Nelsons they bribed a maid to bring them cups and a pot of tea as black as Grandpa drank. Over this brew Ellie could almost hear his voice telling about when he was a lad walking hots at Leopardstown. One night she dozed off and woke later, to find tea spilled on her sheets and Pam asleep with tears on her face. Mopping up her bed she woke Pam.

"Oh, I'm so tired of all this!" Pam wailed. "I hate riding, and this stupid hotel and everything. There hasn't even been time to visit the School of Drama, or have any fun at all. I wish I'd never—"

"Don't say it," Ellie cut in. She too was worn out and afraid of flying into a senseless quarrel. She knew that when people were tired enough they might speak cruelly, and she had a suspicion Pam had been about to say, "I wish I'd never met you.

There were good times too, and funny ones. From pure nerves the girls were ready to laugh hysterically at the feeblest jokes. One day Dolly confessed she used to think scratching a horse meant exactly that, easing its itch. And once Andy teased Pam till she got so flustered that she in turn called him "Sweetheart." Then there was the evidently nearsighted lady on the street who asked

Ellie for the time, ". . . if you please, sonny." Most comical, one evening when Pam had changed in a hurry for dinner, her petticoat fell down as she crossed the lobby. Ellie heard a sort of squeak behind her and turned to see Pam standing red-faced in a circle of white. Pam appeared to be paralyzed and Ellie became convulsed with giggles. "Pick it up!" she gasped.

With her lips Pam made frantic but soundless motions which seemed to mean "Help!" She sat down on the floor, spreading her skirt to cover the petticoat. A bell boy sprang to help her up. She shrank from him as if he had intended to hit her.

Ellie stood by, doubled with laughter. "Get up and walk away," she hissed, ignoring the bell boy. "Pretend it isn't yours."

But poor Pam was too embarrassed to move. She might have sat there forever if the bell boy hadn't been called away. Then she leaped to her feet, snatched up the petticoat and fled to the elevator.

That evening at dinner Dolly scolded the girls. Her baby-doll face was about as fierce as a rosebud. "You two are overdoing it," she said. "Talk about mental class maniacs! You'll make yourselves sick, working so hard."

"Oh, we like work," Ellie answered.

"We love it," Pam said impishly. In a red wool dress with her hair brushed shiny she was awfully pretty.

Ellie thought, as often before, that she herself looked awkward in a dress. She had decided to wear only tailored clothes when she grew up. She would have a good shape for suits. Now she said, "I wish the finals were the last day of the show instead of the first. We'd have more time, and time helps. Every day Pam and Challenger get better together."

"And of course you two would like to stay through the whole show," Jim suggested. Because of expenses and school, they planned to leave for home right after the finals.

Ellie listened absently, thinking of Challenger and of his rivals. She had met some of the other medal finalists, a nice bunch. In fact so far all the horsemen here were nice and made a fuss over her and Pam. They were tickled that the team of trainer-and-rider had come such a distance, and called them "the kids from the West." Pete Dokes, their old rival, was here too from California, but he was to show a local borrowed horse. Challenger was the horse who had come the farthest distance.

Over dessert, Pam was telling the plan of taking one day off, the day before the finals. That was always Grandpa's advice, to relax or play just before your biggest class. They would do some sight-seeing, maybe go to the theater, surely visit the School of Drama. They wanted to see the terrific view from the Empire State

Building and the prehistoric horses in the Museum of Natural History. Challenger too would need a change. Out of her thoughts, Ellie spoke aloud. "Not that he's tired or sour. Or homesick. He's beginning to enjoy himself, now that he knows his way around."

Jim was watching her with a smile. "You and your horse!" he exclaimed. "How can you possibly know what he thinks?"

There it was again, Ellie thought, people not believing she knew Challenger's mind, and his fears and likes and hates, and all in his heart. "I don't know how I know," she said slowly, staring at Jim without really seeing him. "It's just something inside me that makes me—makes me understand him. I understand other horses, any horse I'm around long enough. It's like being inside him, as if I am him, seeing from his eyes and reasoning with his brains and having his feelings . . . Oh, I can't explain, except—it's so *natural*, knowing what he thinks!" She looked around at the smiling faces and suddenly smiled back. They were swell, and it didn't matter if they had no idea what she meant. What mattered was that she had this thing, whatever it was. It must be a mixture of instinct and sympathy and what she had learned. Mostly it must be loving horses so much that she would die without them. Maybe having it made her sort of peculiar, but she wouldn't have traded it for anything.

Next morning, schooling, she tried to concentrate more on Pam than on Challenger. Pam sure looked right, trim and at the same time graceful. Maybe her love of acting helped her. At any rate she was successfully playing the part of an excellent rider. Of course such a good horse made her look better than she really was. She hadn't much strength or judgment, maybe not much nerve, but as long as Challenger went well she would go well, and would look just about perfect. It was up to him. Having realized all along how much depended on him, Ellie thought of him rather than Pam as the medal finalist.

Certainly the two were getting used to each other, each learning patience with the other and each growing able to guess pretty well what the other was going to do. Challenger had shortened his stride a bit for Pam, since she kept him slower than Ellie had. Pam in turn was trying to give him enough rein over his fences. Occasionally she didn't and then he would snatch for it. And occasionally he took too much hold. But Ellie could see daily improvements and a growing bond between them. They were so friendly now that she had to remind herself not to act jealous. Once when Pam offered to feed him she objected. "No. He likes me to do it. After all—"

"Oh yes," Pam said quickly. "After all he is yours. You feed him."

That made Ellie ashamed. "No, go ahead. All the better that you two get real friendly." But she had to turn and walk out of sight while Pam took charge. That night she dreamed Pam had stolen Challenger. With the absurdness of dreams Pam kept saying, "Well, we have to go in there fighting." But not with each other, Ellie resolved when she woke.

Thursday morning was only two days before the show would open with the medal finals. The girls headed for the Garden, determined to make this last schooling their best. It had to be faultless.

"Then tomorrow a whole day off," said Pam as they hurried along the still sleepy streets. "But I don't think I'm going to enjoy my holiday."

"Rubbish," Ellie said stoutly but inwardly she agreed.

"I'll probably be sick," Pam went on.

"That's fine," Ellie answered. "Remember Grandpa always says it's good to be keyed up a little."

"A little!"

"Hey, watch out!" Ellie held Pam back to wait for a green light.

"I'd just as soon be run over," Pam said so gloomily that Ellie wondered if possibly Pam really was getting sick. She had heard that sometimes people practically made themselves sick to avoid something they dreaded.

Oh death, she thought, wouldn't that be just dandy! As if tomorrow wouldn't be bad enough, and then all Saturday to live through, for the show wouldn't open until eight in the evening. Luckily they would have to pack for home on Saturday, and too Ellie could spend most of the day with the horses. Challenger would need only walking that morning since he would be jumping at night. She also had accepted a couple of braiding jobs. Pam would visit first the hairdresser, then Dolly's family. Ellie had suggested these visits with a vague idea that a day apart would be a good thing.

Walking along, she nearly smiled to hear herself repeating with Pam, "Brush, red gate, picket, post-and-rails, red gate again, stone wall." There were five fences in the ring, which meant jumping six times by taking the red gate twice, and of course all this in a figure eight. At least Pam wouldn't forget her course as she had at Palm Springs. That couldn't happen twice—could it?

Beside her, deep in thought, Pam said, "Don't interrupt. I'm in chapter five of that miserable book of charts. The Leg, Parts of. The cannon bone stops exactly where?"

"Exactly here," Ellie answered. She stooped to touch the front of her ankle, almost forcing the man behind her to leapfrog over her.

"Mm, yes. Now I'll rehearse equipment." With eyes closed to concentrate, Pam collided with a hurrying woman.

"Well, really," snapped the woman.

"Well really yourself!" Ellie retorted in irritation.

Entering the Garden they ran into Andy, who took one look at Ellie and said, "Listen, Freckles. So you don't win. So what? So in a hundred years who cares?" A great comfort he was!

The true comfort came from this morning's schooling. Ellie's spirits rose to a peak while she watched from the alley that separated the box seats from the ring. She placed herself where if she had reached in she could have touched the post-and-rails fence during the class. It would be the hardest fence to take because of the sharp turn leading into it. This had been her chosen coaching spot where Pam in passing caught her eye and her advice. The ring was crowded as always, but Ellie felt that even in that mob a spectator would pick out her team as tops. The medal course wasn't set up now. There were only four fences on the rail, but Challenger tackled them so professionally that he made Pam appear to have almost perfect horsemanship.

Ellie glowed with pride at the results of her training. She noticed others watching the pair as Pam pulled up to loosen her girth before taking the rail again at a walk.

Passing the coaching spot Pam glanced down inquiringly, then broke into a big answering smile. There was no need for words. In fact Ellie could hardly have spoken because there was a kind of lump in her throat. It might be crazy to feel suddenly so happy, but look at this beautiful hunter who had come up the long hard way from being a sort of Cinderella horse. How could you see him, so good and so honest after what he'd been through, without getting all melted inside!

She was startled from her reflections by a man's voice behind her. "Didn't I judge that big chestnut at Palm Springs?"

Turning, Ellie recognized Howard Prescott. "Why of course," he exclaimed. "I remember you too. Patrick Sayre's granddaughter."

"That's my horse you just saw," she said, trying to keep her tone casual. Would he make some comment on Challenger's performance? No, of course not. Judges saved their opinions till they were judging.

He merely repeated, "Your horse . . . named Challenger, I believe." So he remembered! His eyes went thoughtfully from Ellie to Pam and back to Ellie. Evidently he was remembering more. "How is it you're not riding him?" he said. "Unless I'm mistaken you're eligible for the hunt seat finals."

"Yes, I'm eligible," she answered. "That is, we consider it's Challenger who's eligible. He's the important one, you know. It doesn't matter so much who rides him as long as he . . ." She hesitated, fearing to sound as if she were asking for favors. "As long as he does well," she finished.

Mr. Prescott was smiling. "In that case," he said, "I should think you would show him yourself. This girl on him is a nice rider, but between you and me you're a better one."

Someone interrupted then, ending the conversation. Ellie went off with increased satisfaction. She hoped it wasn't disloyal to Pam, her being glad that a few people knew she was still Challenger's best rider. All the better if Pam didn't know it, or the Mortons and Nelsons, who weren't real horsemen. But she couldn't help knowing it herself. And the others who knew were the ones who mattered—Grandpa surely, and Mr. Prescott, and Challenger. Somehow their knowing lightened the weight of her sacrifice.

On the way to the stalls she began to wonder what Mr. Prescott had meant by calling Pam a "nice" rider. Did he consider her good, very good, fair or what? It was impossible to guess. It struck Ellie only now that he should have recognized Pam. He had placed her first in her equitation class at Palm Springs. His forgetting could mean she hadn't impressed him enough. Or, Ellie hoped, it could mean Pam had improved beyond recognition.

As she went on toward the stalls, she was disturbed by another worry. Maybe this morning's schooling shouldn't have been quite so successful. Obviously no one could always do well. Horsemen claimed they expected bad luck now and then. Some tried to ward it off with charms like rabbits' feet. Others ignored it, or joked or worked extra hard. Still there were days when fences fell over seemingly by themselves. There were days when riders fell off or horses fell down. Some got up and walked away. Some got up but didn't walk very well. Some didn't get up at all. It would be better to have such a day behind than just around the next corner.

12. The Finals

CHALLENGER too would be waking about now, Ellie thought on Saturday morning, the Saturday of the finals. The bedroom window showed only faint light, but electric lights would be bright in the Garden's underworld. From tack rooms stable boys would emerge, tousled with sleep and grumbling at the early hour. Horses would scramble to their feet, shake, yawn, stretch and nicker. Radios would blare out the news, or more often the results of yesterday's racing. Faucets would gush, shovels scrape, brooms swish. Pans and buckets would clatter. Wires would snap on opening hay bales, tin quart measures would scoop into grain for those who could eat before exercising. Shortly the trainers would appear from their hotels. Then the boys would step livelier and grumble more for being hollered at. The coffee stand would open, mingling its cozy smell with all the other smells that probably made the background of all horse shows throughout the world.

Over his stall door Challenger would be watching, listening, knowing this was his day. He wouldn't be nervous exactly, but he would feel the beginning of tenseness that would build up little by little with the hours until he was just right. There was a point where a horse was sort of stirred up, yet not jittery. Under that point he wouldn't be quite ready; over it he would be too excited. He had to be like a wire strung taut; with a fraction less strain it would sag, with a fraction more it would snap.

Ellie sat up cautiously to look at Pam. All she saw was a sleeping hump. That was fine, for they had planned that this morning Ellie would go alone to the Garden while Pam kept her various appointments. Pam would probably sleep late after yesterday's sight-seeing. In a way Ellie envied her, able to postpone thinking of the trial ahead. She could tell from familiar sensations inside that her own nerves weren't postponing. There was that sort of sickness in her stomach. She swallowed and found that already her throat was tightening. She better leave her retainer off today so it wouldn't gag her. Yet even though she expected to feel pretty awful during the next fourteen hours, she wouldn't have missed a minute of them. They would hold at least one consolation—she had done her best. There wasn't much more she could do now toward winning. At this late date it would be silly to put more pressure on schooling. Tonight's results were practically out of her hands. They were up to Challenger and Pam. As she tiptoed about the lightening room among packed and half-packed suitcases, it struck her that by ignoring her stomach she might even be able to enjoy this last day in New York. She would if her mind would ignore the figure eight course it kept picturing, including the red gate in the center which had to be jumped twice at an angle.

With her mackinaw zipped up snug and her hands in the pockets she jogged along the sidewalks. It was fun to copy Challenger's trot, until people's stares embarrassed her. He would be expecting her now, not worried, but like a child who is used to breakfast at a certain time. He would be standing close to the partition that separated him from Flight, and probably he would be consoling her for having to miss the finals, although she was completely well again. Most likely they would agree that in spite of all New York's glamor they would be glad to see again the soft green hills of home. Especially, Challenger would say, if he could return to California a winner. Placing at all among all these Easterners would be fine, but there was something about a blue ribbon. . . . There was that heartbeating moment when you lined up with the other horses, and the big voice like the end of the world said "Announcing the Awards," and then your name was called and you alone stepped out—

Not so fast, Ellie warned herself, slowing her steps and her imagination as she reached the Garden. How familiar it was, after being so awesome a week ago. Only a week? It seemed that a month had passed since the Santa Fe train pulled into Grand Central Station. Yet it hadn't been long enough. One more week, even an extra day, and Challenger would be that much more used to Pam. It was still Ellie he expected in the saddle, just as now he expected her footsteps and welcomed them with outstretched head and mumbled greetings. With almost guilty pleasure Ellie knew that no matter who fed or cared for him or rode or won or lost on him, he would never doubt that he was hers.

"Would you, honey?" she said, going into his stall.

He answered with an impatient nudge which meant, Of course not—what a stupid question!

"Oh, it's food you're interested in. All right, just a minute while I check on Flight. I said just a minute, you don't have to shove me all over the place!"

Next door Flight also was hungry. "Since you too will only be walked," Ellie told her, "you can both eat before work." It was good to see the mare enjoying her breakfast, and not surprising that Challenger soon turned from his. That was his habit on important days, whether he caught uneasiness from Ellie or from the other horses or by his own instinct. As usual on such days he grabbed a mouthful of hay, then whirled to look into the aisle, dropping more hay than he ate. He was impatient for grain, and plunged his jaws into the pan. He gulped a few mouthfuls, then turned to his door again, spilling the grain instead of chewing it. Ellie stood by silently, knowing nothing she could do would coax him to eat. This was part of his own method of charging himself up for tonight's test, and it would be useless to cross him. When Andy came by, jaunty in his turtle-neck sweater, and invited Ellie to breakfast, she felt just like Challenger. The thought of food made her stomach squirm.

"Stall walkin', huh?" he said, inspecting her with understanding eyes.

"Sort of," she admitted, and warmed by his sympathy she went on. "I've discovered it's loads harder to be a trainer than a rider. When you're on a horse, at least you're doing something. But trainers knock themselves out to get another person and a horse ready, and then at the important moment they have to stand by helplessly and watch."

"Tough, sweatin' it out," Andy agreed. "But cheer up, Freckles. What if you'd trained a million-dollar race horse and then had to look on while your jock gets left at the post?"

"Honestly," Ellie said crossly, "you have the weirdest ideas of encouragement."

Leading Challenger today was like handling dynamite. With his mind distracted and spirits keen, Ellie didn't dare take him into the ring. Horses jumping and galloping all around might tempt him to pull loose. It would have been easier to ride, but since he had grown used to Pam, Ellie had faithfully stayed off him. She wouldn't take a chance of confusing any signals or hints he and Pam might be using even unconsciously. They walked up and down the aisles, and she wondered how many miles of cement her poor feet had trudged this week.

Then there was Flight to lead, also quite a task because Flight was feeling skittish again. When both had been walked, Ellie brought out her saddle soap, silver polish and cloths and gave all of Pam's tack a thorough cleaning. Pam had promised to do the same with her clothes. The black boots must be shined, the white stock ironed stiff, coat and britches brushed. Her hunting cap and gloves must be spotless.

While Ellie worked she kept glancing at Challenger, who was watching her restively. He knew it would soon be his turn for a grooming. She decided he ought to relax at least for a while and might do it better without her.

"I'll go see if it's too early to braid for those people," she told him. "Try to doze a little, or something. Isn't it silly, you and Pam and me all having to be separated so we won't get on each others' nerves!"

On the way to braiding she stopped at the phone booth and called Pam, just to make sure she was all right.

"I can't find my stock pin," Pam said irritably. "Where did you put it?"

"I didn't touch it," Ellie said. "It must be there some-where. Maybe it's packed in one of our suitcases."

"It isn't. I dumped everything out."

"Oh, no!" There was a pause, while outside the phone booth a man stood tapping his foot impatiently. Ellie could only suggest, "Look again."

"It's easy for you to say that," Pam accused her. "Why don't you borrow one for me?"

"Who from?" Ellie was trying not to see the man looking at his watch.

"How do I know?" Pam snapped. "That's your worry."

Oh, this was crazy. They were getting nowhere, ex-cept into a quarrel. Ellie said desperately, "All right, I'll borrow one. And I'll come to the hotel around three." Silence. "Pam? I'll show up at three. You'll be there?"

"I guess so," Pam replied, and Ellie left the booth

with a nagging new worry that Pam was upset by something more than her missing stock pin.

Borrowing another one turned out to be a problem. Ellie hardly knew the other riders, and Grandpa disapproved so strongly of borrowing that she hesitated to ask. When she did ask she found that the medal contestants naturally would all be using their own pins tonight. Somebody's mother at last came to the rescue with an extra one. It was an insecure little pin which gave Ellie visions of its opening and stabbing Pam through the throat when she was in mid-air.

She managed to spend two hours braiding two hunters. The fact that she was doing it for tonight's finals made her feel rather treacherous as she pocketed her pay. Next she forced herself to have a glass of milk and a doughnut at the coffee stand. There she heard a couple discussing the finalists. They said such nice things about "the California rider" that she gloated until she discovered the rider they meant was Pete Dokes.

Her watch showed noon when she went back to Challenger. It was time for his bath. Afterward she must scrape and walk him dry, and with luck by that time it would be near two. The stables would be at their quietest, with most everyone gone for a nap. The great building would seem to be holding its breath between the day's efforts and their goal, the night's climax. Challenger too would rest, while Ellie spent an hour or so with Pam. Then she would come back to tie him so he wouldn't eat before jumping, not that that was likely. She would braid him, the slickest job of her life, and grease his hoofs, and brush and rub him till he was absolutely gorgeous. Last of all she would saddle and bridle him and hold him for Pam. He would look not at Pam but at her. What if his nerve failed him at the final second? Still she would have to stand back and say "Go ahead." And then—it would be up to him.

The next few hours went according to schedule, so that it was close to three when Ellie arrived at the Sportsman. Crossing the lobby, now so familiar, she realized that her next trip from the revolving doors to the elevator would be late tonight. It would be all over. She remembered wondering on the train with Pam whether their return journey would be sad or happy. "We'll soon know," she said to herself as she went toward their room. "Meanwhile I better get Pam in a good mood if I'm a halfway smart trainer."

At their door she put on a cheerful expression. But inside the room cheer gave way to dismay. The room was a wreck. Pam had meant it all right when she said she had "dumped everything out" of the carefully packed suitcases. The oddest sight of all was Pam herself. She was dressed for her class—five hours early—all but her boots. From head to knees she looked terribly stylish, although her dark eyes were stormy. The contrast with bare legs and feet was comical. Seeing Ellie, she announced, "It's all over. I can't show tonight."

"What!"

Pam pointed dramatically at her boots, which she had flung aside. "I can't get into them. I must have grown." She started to remove her coat. "It's lucky I decided to try everything on early. Now we know. It's no use. Finished." Although she was being theatrical, underneath she sounded really upset.

She had tried every trick used by horsemen, she said, to pull on the boots, all in vain. In the interval since she had last worn them, plainly her legs had grown. "Not fatter," she said with dignity. "It's muscles."

The combination of dignity and bare feet made Ellie want to giggle. Across the disorder she stared at Pam. "Did you try powder?" she asked. "Soap?"

Pam nodded with the finality of despair and began to take off her shirt. "I even rubbed my legs with a lemon," she said. "Though why a lemon would do any—"

The picture was too much for Ellie. She collapsed laughing on the nearest bed.

"I really don't see—" Pam began coldly, and then collapsed too across the other bed, now wearing only elegant buff britches and her bra.

They had a lovely refreshing interval of laughing like fools. This wasn't solving the problem though. At last, pulling herself together, Ellie suggested ice. Ice made things shrink, didn't it?

"My poor legs," Pam wailed.

With great daring Ellie telephoned the bar downstairs and ordered a bowl of ice.

Half an hour later they agreed wearily that the operation had been a success. It might have been the mixed recipe of powder, soap, lemon and ice that made Pam's legs slippery, or the girls' combined strength. At any rate inch by inch and grunt by groan, finally the boots went on.

The next excitement was caused by letters pushed under the door. Ellie pounced on them, one from Pam's parents, one from Grandpa. This one contained, besides instructions, some hints that Grandpa had grown pretty fond of Mrs. Bannister. "Don't those Mrs. Bannister days seem ages ago?" Pam said reflectively.

"Yes, and remember when we used to collect stuffed animals and dolls? And the day we smoked secretly hiding from Grandpa?"

"I do think," Pam remarked, "that we've improved a lot since then."

But already Ellie was losing interest in these ordinarily fascinating subjects. Her thoughts were reaching toward

Challenger. He must be wondering where she was. Grandpa would understand.

While Pam read aloud the "good luck" messages from her letter, Ellie changed into jodhpurs and checked jacket. A trainer should look neat. While she dressed she tried to decide whether to say any more about tonight's class. Encouragement, warnings, reminders—surely she and Pam had gone over every single detail dozens of times. Still she asked, half-joking, "You do know the course, don't you?"

"Brush, red gate, picket, post-and-rails, red gate again, stone wall."

"And you will remember to give him lots of rein over his fences? He'll need most at the post-and-rails like we said, because those darn poles roll off so easily. And it's after that nasty turn. But the main thing, Pam, sit still. That's the best way, don't forget, to help Challenger help you."

"I'll remember everything," Pam promised. "Now you go ahead. And don't worry, I won't be late. I'll take a cab, or Dolly and Jim will bring me. I couldn't walk unless my legs thaw."

Still Ellie stared at her uncertainly. "What about supper?" she asked. Then both together said, "No." She looked back from the door. Pam's face suddenly was less confident as she asked, "How does he feel? I mean, inside himself like you say, he'll be ready, won't he?"

"He'll be ready," Ellie answered and went out quickly. If she had any doubt it wasn't of her horse but of her jockey.

She had been right about Challenger's missing her. He recognized her step even sooner than usual and called to her with a neigh rather than a nicker. It was funny though, as soon as she stood near him he stopped paying attention to her. Plainly satisfied now that she was here, he turned his mind to the night's business. What made him more distant was that he seemed somehow to have grown. Standing in his bronze statue pose he dwarfed Ellie. It was as if unintentionally he snubbed her. It struck her that a mother might feel this way the day she realized her child was grown up. The child who used to need her tender care all at once had outgrown it. A good mother would know she musn't fuss over him any longer. She would be glad to see him independent because it would mean she had done a fine job of raising him. Hey, thought Ellie, mothers are trainers too. . . . But good grief, this was no time to be daydreaming. She had better get busy. Everyone else was busy in all the aisles, judging from the noise of preparations. That noise was different than it had been earlier. Voices were sharper, steps faster. The very air, closer now, was

charged with mounting tension. You could smell tanbark as if the ring above were pressing nearer.

All this, Ellie found, wasn't very good for a person's
stomach. Also it made fingers slippery with perspiration.
It took will-power to steady hers for braiding Challenger,
more so because these had to be absolutely perfect braids
—twelve tight and even ones for the mane, but the tail
not so tight that separate hairs would pull. Absorbed in
the difficult task, she was hardly aware of the people,
some in evening clothes, who stopped at the stall door to
watch. They made flattering remarks about Challenger,
who ignored them. He was staring off above them,
listening to the faint hum and shuffle upstairs. His nostrils
snuffed in and out experimentally and the veins swelled
where the sweat of nerves dampened his fine-skinned
neck. Even these strangers seeing him couldn't doubt he
knew what was ahead. What they saw in her, Ellie
thought, was on the contrary unimpressive. Her shirt
sleeves were rolled up, wire and scissors stuck out of her
pockets, lengths of thread were held between her teeth
and a frown of effort showed between her eyes.

After braiding she brushed Challenger all over, then
polished him with the rubrag. His coat smelled lovely
since his bath. She trimmed the long hairs from his ears
and nostrils, picked out his feet, greased his hoofs and

ran the sponge again over his white diamond and stockings. She was standing back to admire him when she heard the first notes of the band tuning up overhead. Then here came Pam with the Nelsons. Dolly and Jim seemed a bit bewildered at being jostled by busy horsemen whose pace increased with the passing minutes. With no warm-up area, the aisles had become jammed. Coaching riders, even watching them warm up, would be impossible. In any case Ellie knew that unless Pam was ready now she never would be.

Pam was pale. Compared to Challenger's height and might she looked horribly dainty. She didn't smile, only asked, "Is it time to saddle?"

Knowing from experience, Ellie answered, "No, not for at least fifteen minutes, since our number's last. Why don't you go help Dolly and Jim find their seats? By the time you get back we'll hear the first call."

The others left, and she was alone with Challenger. They didn't need to touch each other or to talk. Everything between them had been said. They just stood together waiting quietly until the voice of the announcer sounded. "First call for the hunt seat medal finals. Hunt seat medal class, first call. You have twenty minutes."

From then on things happened rapidly, as in one of those nightmares where you're swept along faster and faster with no power to slow down. While Ellie was saddling, Pam appeared, silent, white and determined. She put on her number, the one to jump last. The long wait was going to be tough for her, Ellie thought. Challenger stood for Pam to mount, but it was Ellie he looked at with wise and steadfast eyes—different eyes, a different horse from what he had been two years ago. With bold steps he left to warm up in the aisles before climbing the ramp. She watched him go and she thought with a funny sort of ache, why—why, Challenger had grown up!

Upstairs was the same dream of being swept along, but here the current sparkled with all the glitter of the famous show's opening night. Clutching her exhibitor's pass, Ellie was drawn with the crowd toward the seating area. Behind a dressed-up lady who smelled heavenly, she passed through a curtained entrance into the box seat section. All around her people in evening clothes were talking, laughing, greeting friends. Below lay the ring, a breath-taking expanse of fresh tanbark, smooth as a lake. The course was set, five gleaming fences which dared a rider to spoil their perfection. They were picture fences, the brush unbelievably green, the picket vivid in every point, the post-and-rails dazzling white, each stone of the wall clean cut. In the cross of the figure eight the red paint on the gate glistened as if it weren't yet dry. Still moving in her nightmare, Ellie pushed her way gradually downward until at last she reached the alley skirting the ring. She stationed herself in her usual coaching spot almost within reach of the post-and-rails. Even this place tonight was unfamiliar, not private but open and bare to the lights and the noise of eight thousand people finding seats in the vast auditorium.

In the middle of the ring stood a bugler at attention in red coat and high silk hat. As Ellie watched with fascination he raised his bugle and blew the note which officially opened the show. The manager spoke a few welcoming words. He introduced several celebrities, including New York's mayor, then Howard Prescott and the saddle horse judge. Next:

"Ladies and gentlemen, our National Anthem."

The lights dimmed, except a single beam focused on the flag draped high against one wall. A great rustle spread as everyone stood to the strains of the "Star-Spangled Banner." In the dark, Ellie shivered. Her head filled with the bitter smell of tanbark which always meant excitement. Her throat tightened and she fought the urge to swallow, afraid that she wouldn't be able to. It was a panicky sensation, followed as usual by her heart going in big jerks. Just when she couldn't resist trying to swallow, although she knew it would strangle her, the lights sprang on again. Talk and laughter rose as the crowd settled, with a flutter of programs and here and there the flash of jewels or the flare of match to cigarette.

Immediately the loudspeaker announced the medal class finals. Mr. Prescott entered the ring and stood near the red gate. The ring crew in white squatted at one side below the rail, ready to set up fallen fences. The number one rider was called. The gate swung open. The class was under way.

In a sort of trance Ellie watched the contestants one after another flying around with almost faultless performances. Not really faultless, but their mistakes were such terribly small ones! Maybe this one was a shade fast, that one a shade slow, or his timing not quite certain or his posture not just perfect. She would have given anything to know what Mr. Prescott marked on his score card with occasional pencil stabs, seeming hardly to take his eyes from the riders. In vain she tried to guess his criticisms. Everyone's turn came so fast that it was like watching a merry-go-round of horses—black, brown, bay, gray and chestnut, carrying black coated, black booted figures, all with starched white stocks and trim hunting caps, all looking grim. The only one common fault Ellie could see, a fault scarcely visible, was uneven speed. It must be because of the angles at which they had to jump to take six fences within the figure eight. But then, how much did pace matter to Mr. Prescott? Or how much did he score it against Pete Dokes that after hitting the stone wall Pete looked back to see if it fell? It didn't fall, but teetered for a long agonizing moment until the crowd let out a big breath and someone in the stands yelled, "Lucky dog!"

Ellie had stood as if rooted for so long that she didn't recognize Pam's number when it was called. It was a voice in a box behind her that made her jump. "There's the last horse." Gripping the rail, her hands began to tremble and words went round and round in her head. "Do it, do it, do it." Distractedly she heard more voices. "The California horse," "A beauty," "How well he moves," and oh, death,! "Too big to make that turn for the post-and-rails."

It was so unreal to *watch* Challenger show, that Ellie found herself imagining she was on him. In a weird way she could feel him under her, stepping in with his long stride, studying the course while he walked his circle. Ahead of her his neck was a shiny arch topped by twelve perfect braids. The clean smell of his coat mixed with the smell of clean leather. His gleaming shoulders pumped in powerful rhythm, his ears pricked eagerly. Under his breath he snorted, just gently to show he felt good. He was measuring the fences, knowing he would have no trouble if his rider let him run on and jump free. He had reached the peak of readiness.

Ellie's knees tightened, her hands steadied invisible reins as Challenger took up his trot. She clucked and leaned forward, and he was galloping bold and true for the center of the brush. Not too fast, don't jump too big, she prayed. If you land too far over you'll pass your angle for the red gate. There, the brush flashed under us, that crazy green color. Now straighten and bear right— easy, easy—don't rush. More rein, *rein*, Pam! Sit down, sit down, don't shift your weight, don't breathe, let him—let him . . . Don't you see what he's doing, don't you see?

Ellie had guessed what Challenger meant to do. He was going to take those three fences—brush, red gate, picket—like an in-and-out. Without changing pace he had landed, put in three strides, measured his take off and was soaring up again and over in one smooth flow-ing arc. If Pam just sat still, if she didn't—Oh, it made her look beautiful! She was a model of horsemanship, her legs firm, heels down, her back hollowed, elbows close, chin up, hands supple. And she had caught on, she wasn't interfering. Oh good girl, she was helping Challenger to help her!

He was airborne now over the red gate and floating down. There wasn't a sound except of hoofs on the tan-bark they scattered in sharp-scented spurts. White stockings checked barely a fraction for the picket, then rose again and silently skimmed its painted points. Over the three fences they had made three giant scallops, the only performance with unchanged speed.

Please, please, Ellie prayed, all mixed up with being Challenger and Pam and herself, and even Grandpa proud of her training. Behind her, people were whispering. The stands were tense, so quiet that single sounds came loud: a cough clear up in the bleachers, the squeak of Pam's boot on the saddle skirt, and Challenger's blowing, which meant he felt on top of the world.

"Look out, Pam," Ellie begged silently, for next was the hateful post-and-rails after the turn. All at the same time she watched Mr. Prescott's face and Pam, who must be dying of nerves while she put on this tremendous show, and Challenger eyeing the post-and-rails.

Suddenly Ellie stiffened with fright. Something was wrong with him! Nobody else could have told, but she knew, she just knew. During instants that seemed ages she sensed he was in trouble. Then it flashed on her, he needed more rein. Pam didn't realize it. She had forgotten it was here he would have to have more rein to get a run after collecting himself on the turn. Then he must jump big, and if she held him he would either pull her from the saddle or roll off a pole. Worse than either, he might have to refuse. That would break his heart.

Ellie wanted to close her eyes, to yell at Pam, to stop

Challenger, anything. Wildly she wanted to halt the class before he lost it. As if she were Challenger, she understood he had to jump, that it was cruel to prevent him. Breeding, training, every instinct in him shouted "Jump." It was against his learning, reason, against his very nature to refuse. From years of work, tonight he could have won. This should have been his night. Yet he was being forced to lose. For no horse could take off with tightened reins. His rider hadn't thrown her heart ahead. He couldn't follow.

Paralyzed, Ellie stared at him. She saw him make his winning move. In the same second that Mr. Prescott's pencil darted to his card, in that second Challenger snatched for rein—and got it. A tiny motion, the only one that could have saved him! When Mr. Prescott raised his eyes, Challenger's neck was stretched free, thanks to the added slack. His hocks dug in to spring. He took off. Pam never touched his mouth. She sat with apparent ease, leaned forward exactly in contact, poised while he poised over the fence. They landed with not a splinter off a pole, and the wind of their passage brushed Ellie's face as they swept on.

She knew what would follow, and it did. As before, Challenger took the two angled fences like an in-and-out. With bold precision he flew the red gate, leaped the stone wall, allowed Pam to pull up and left the ring with

the style of a champion. Through tears of joy Ellie saw
that his walk was cocky, and he knew it and didn't care,
because it should be, when a horse had class and bril-
liance and a proud name he'd lived up to!

After that there wasn't much doubt about the awards.

The Finals

In the hacking phase Pam and Challenger looked relaxed and handsome but still worked carefully every step of the way. Then, lined up, Pam was questioned by Mr. Prescott. From his nod, it was plain that she answered correctly.

Ellie scarcely heard the awards because of the applause. Her eyes were blurred, her spine was chilled, her bangs on end. Her heart was pounding and her stomach churned as on a ferris wheel. Later she realized she needn't have heard anything to know that Challenger had won. Nobody needed to be told, because the proof was there for all who had watched the class.

For Ellie, besides proof, was the hint from a faint tune running through her head. It was one a successful trainer might hum, a mournful Irish song called "Farewell, Shamrock Shores."